Café
Britannica

Stephen Carter

Café Britannica

Ten Tales with Tea and Cake

Stephen Cardew

Illustrations by Brode

The Book Guild Ltd

First published in Great Britain in 2018 by
The Book Guild Ltd
9 Priory Business Park
Wistow Road, Kibworth
Leicestershire, LE8 0RX
Freephone: 0800 999 2982
www.bookguild.co.uk
Email: info@bookguild.co.uk
Twitter: @bookguild

Typeset in Minion Pro

Printed and bound in Great Britain by CPI Group (UK) Ltd, Croydon, CR0 4YY

ISBN 978 1912362 073

British Library Cataloguing in Publication Data.
A catalogue record for this book is available from the British Library.

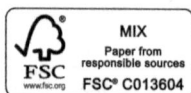

This book is dedicated to my wife, who kept up my motivation levels when they flagged; my family, whose influences are clear in everything I write, and to my grandchildren, who I adore.

Contents

Café Nostalgia

I was driving out on the Chatsworth Road, thinking about some of the things we used to get up to at school, when I saw a sign – one of those hand-painted signs – nailed to a tree: 'Café Nostalgia.' I glanced in the mirror and, seeing not much behind, braked hard and turned sharply up a track on the left. Nothing cafe-like was immediately visible so I got out and ran back to look again at the sign. Yes, it was definitely pointing this way. I got back in the car and made my way slowly up the slight incline, trying to avoid the many potholes.

Cresting the rise, I saw, about 200 yards distant, a medium-sized hut. As I neared, the sign above came into focus:

Café Nostalgia
… where everything's like it used to be

I pulled up beside the building on a dirt patch hollowed by previous tyres and got out. The sound of laughter and hum of gentle conversation greeted me through the open windows. Anticipating the interior, I walked a little more slowly than is my habit towards the door. The door opened outwards and I stepped inside. Arrayed before me was a happy congregation of evenly-spaced, gingham-topped tables, burdened just adequately with menus and cutlery and condiments. Three or four were already occupied and behind a counter, at the far end, stood a smiling woman in her early forties.

'Have a seat, love,' she called. 'Anywhere you like.'

'Thanks,' I replied, and chose a table by the window.

I reached instinctively for the menu but didn't open it. I wanted to savour the situation and paused to look round at Café Nostalgia. Bric-à-brac was everywhere, interspersed with black-and-white photos of smiling folk and posters of 60s films. Fonda and Hopper sat astride unattainably cool choppers. Taylor and Burton brooded over Egyptian politics and Connery caressed himself with the barrel of his Walther PPK. What an era that had been! I wasn't even there, except for the very end of it, but it seemed such a time to be alive. Black Power and white-hot technology. Bra-burning and Playboy bunnies. Winds of change and the Space Race… Men who wanted to change the world and thought they just might. Women who wanted to change men and thought they just might. Girls who just might.

2

I opened the menu. It was a two-sided padded folder, about quarto size. On the left-hand side, were the meals. On the right-hand side, the puddings.

Meals	Puds
Beefburger, chips and beans. Vesta beef curry and rice. Beans on cheese on toast. Fishfinger butties with salad cream. Bacon and egg butty.	Jam roly-poly and custard. Rice pudding with raspberry jam. Chocolate 'golly' whip. Treacle sponge with ice cream. Trifle.

My eyes swam at the bounty of possibility and my mind flew away back to the happy homecoming meals of my childhood. In my reverie, I didn't immediately notice the waitress appear at my side.

'Have you decided?' she asked and beamed broadly.

'I don't know what to have – they're all my favourites,' I said.

'That's what we aim for, love,' she responded and wrote something on her pad.

'What have you written?' I asked.

'Bacon and egg butty, and jam roly-poly. That's right, isn't it?'

'Yes' I said, ' but how…?' My voice trailed off. She was

already marching back to the counter. 'Five minutes,' she called over her shoulder.

I looked over at a man sitting by himself at the next table. He looked familiar but I couldn't quite place where I knew him from. He turned towards me and smiled. 'Lovely, isn't she?' he said and gestured in the direction of the waitress. 'Makes everyone feel right at home.'

'Yes,' I said. 'An amazing menu.' I turned the folder slightly towards him.

'Oh yes,' he said. 'Keeps me coming back for more.'

'What are you having?' I asked.

'The tripe,' he replied, 'with onions.' He pursed his lips and narrowed his eyes momentarily in keen anticipation.

'But that's not…'

'Here you are, then, love,' the waitress cut across my objection. 'Get it while it's hot.'

She placed a dinner plate in front of me with the largest bap I've ever seen sitting in the middle. Poking out from all sides were edges of half-crispy bacon with raincoat-yellow yolk dripping off them.

'Have you got any…?'

'Sauce is already on,' she smiled. 'Now then,' she continued, 'nice cup of tea to go with that…' It wasn't a question but I still nodded. She was off again. I looked over at the man, eyebrows raised in amazement. He just smiled and tilted his head fractionally to one side.

I tried to savour the butty but it was altogether too delicious and I'm afraid I wolfed it down in no time. The waitress wasn't anywhere to be seen and so I thought that I should take the opportunity to have a break before the pudding. Beside the door, stood a jukebox. A grand old Wurlitzer with a rounded front, magnificent in its multi-coloured glass. I looked in the front panel and warmed instantly to the listings: Zeppelin, Crosby, Stills & Nash, Cream, Stones, middle-period Dylan; Curved Air. Not a single track I didn't like and I reached in my pocket for coins. I searched along the top for the slot but found only a pop-up notice saying 'Free Play.' I pushed C7 and wandered back to my table, just as Stephen Stills' acoustic guitar jumped enthusiastically into 'Suite Judy Blue Eyes.'

The opening bars gave way to the opening words, in that way that songs have, but what was strange, this time, was how far the words were sinking into me. Suddenly that song, that oh-so-familiar song, that song that I had listened to, sang along to and even made love to, became a new song, a savoured song, a song shot-through with clarity.

'Don't let the past remind us of what we are not now,' rang out in frail harmony but its very fragility somehow confirmed its truth. That was it. Those croaky, near-falsetto voices were telling me something exactly in tune with this moment. The past that I was steadfastly maintaining, almost worshipping, was actually punishing me. The past was, in fact, not a done deal, not an amiable companion but, instead, a tormentor, a prison, a nemesis. Here, adrift from ordinary life, in Café Nostalgia, at the very moment when the best of the past had come together like a hundred Christmases, I had a sure realisation: it was time, high time, to leave the past behind.

'Here's your pudding.' The words broke through my

epiphany. The waitress smiled as she put a soup plate in front of me, laden with pastry, jam and steaming custard. It was everything I remembered from home, primary school and visits to Auntie Kay's all rolled up into one conglomeration of delight. I dwelt, for a moment, in the eagerness of expectation before picking up the spoon. I raised it to a point half-way between the tabletop and my mouth but held it there, not moving. Below me, in all its shimmering, glutinous, sweet glory, lay jam roly-poly. Jam roly-poly and custard. The pudding which, above all others, I would crave. The pudding which, more than any other, brought such filling satisfaction to my belly. The pudding which, more than almost anything else, perfectly encapsulated my childhood. The spoon hovered, held in perfect tension between old temptation and new resolution.

***

As I drove away from Cafe Nostalgia, I thought back over what had just happened. I asked for the bill and the waitress told me it came to 'seven-and-six' which, although those words seemed familiar, I decided meant £13. She was flummoxed when I opened my wallet and asked me if I had any change, instead. When I reached into my pocket and brought out a handful of coins, she picked out the 50p piece.

'That covers it,' she said.

It seemed far too little to me and I protested but she

was adamant that 50p was more than enough and that 'half-a-crown' was a very generous tip. She thanked me profusely, smiled the warmest of smiles and wished me a happy future. That was odd.

I drove back down the track, looking for, but not finding, the potholes which had seemed fairly frequent on the drive in. I was soon back turning left onto the Chatsworth Road. The road was quiet and opened out and I soon found myself picking up speed. When I looked at the clock, I saw that I was doing 55mph. Normally, I never exceed 40mph but this felt good, and strangely, it felt right.

I remembered that I had errands to run – stamps from the Post Office, euros from the travel agent's, some fresh bread and that nice pâté we both like from Adcock's – but I decided they could wait. The car's speed was seductive and the road seemed to have no end. It was the moment to go wherever the car was going, the moment to let go, the moment to simply allow.

The car seemed to be almost driving itself but, even as I thought that, I knew also that I was in complete control. I felt dominant and majestic behind the wheel and the engine's thrust became synchronised to my foot. I slowed into bends, rode smoothly through the apex and pulled powerfully out of them. When braking was necessary, I did it without drama or jolting. When it was time to push the rev counter up, I accelerated with a harmony of co-ordination and effort I had not experienced for many years. *This* was driving.

At the next roundabout, I swung all the way round,

noting with satisfaction, the minutest squealing of the tyres, and headed back towards town. The traffic was light and, very soon, I found myself steering smoothly among increasingly commercial buildings, through the densest of them, with lights on green, and then heading out on the dual carriageway, towards the motorway.

'M1… 5' read the signboard and I realised that I would have to make a decision. Feeling, once more, the magnificent buoyancy of possibility, I resolved to leave it to chance – heads, northbound, tails, southbound. With my left hand, I retrieved a pound coin from the slot beside the handbrake, and managed to both spin it and catch it without looking. I tried not to feel smug but only partly succeeded. I looked in my hand. Tails.

The car purred down the slip road and flew out onto the motorway, 'The Ride of the Valkyries' playing loudly in my imagination. I was instantly riding alongside Robert Duvall, in that helicopter gunship, taking on multi-armed form. 'Now I am become Death,' said the prince, 'destroyer of worlds,' and I was that god, able now to destroy the motorway.

I swooped into the outside lane and set off downhill towards 100mph. Cars scattered pleasingly, their drivers aware, no doubt, of the approach of Death and anxious to postpone their own culling. I flew on past lorries, past white vans, past cars towing caravans, past motorcyclists and, very satisfyingly, past a Mustang vying with an Impreza. Above their din, I was nothing more than whispering death. 'Bye,' I mouthed.

Past Junction 28, lay, perhaps, the greatest

concentration of gantry-mounted speed cameras in the Western world. The Highways Agency had, in their wisdom and against all the advice of road traffic experts, decided to widen the motorway to four lanes right down as far as Junction 25. But, to ensure that no-one would be able to take advantage of the increased surface capacity, had installed more speed cameras than you could shake a spray-can at. In my life, until now, this would have constituted more than adequate intimidation to keep me tied and true to its 70mph diktat. Today, not! Today was new me. Today was Ton-up Me.

I pushed down on the throttle and felt the car surge forward once more. The needle pushed on clockwise, cresting 100 easily, on a downslope, and even hitting 110. The exhilaration was electric as I realised that the pedal was on the carpet. This car could do no more to prove its master's bidding and I was glad. I was at the limit.

The fourteen miles to Junction 25 was covered in eight minutes, the same amount of time it had taken me to get from 29 to 28. Four junctions, a little over twenty miles, in sixteen minutes. I exited, swung back round the elevated roundabout and headed back northbound. Of course, now, it was necessary to improve upon that time and I determined to get back in 15 minutes. There might be knots of traffic to circumvent. There might be oil on the carriageway. There might be wild horses galloping in loose formation along the hard shoulder. In short, there might very well be hell to pay but I was getting back in fifteen minutes.

I did.

***

Four days later, a brown envelope fell onto the doormat. It was a notice of impending prosecution, from the Court. Inside was confirmation of the police's intention to prosecute me for travelling at speeds in excess of those permitted on the M1 motorway between junctions 27 and 26 and between junctions 26 and 25 and between junctions 27 and 28 on the day in question. However, I could avoid any such nastiness by accepting a punishment of six penalty points on my licence and a fine of £1,250.

I smiled.

A small price to pay for getting my life back.

Never Judge a Book

The exterior of Inchstar Books was so familiar to Peter that he scarcely noticed it. He mounted the two steps and reached instinctively for the brass latch. He pushed down and started forward, in anticipation of entry, expecting to see Giles on his usual perch. Instead, his shoulder banged clumsily into the half-glazed door, which failed to open, and he stood rebuffed. He tried the handle again but it was clear the door was locked.

'At this time?' he thought to himself, glancing at his watch to confirm it was, as usual, 10.15am. He put his hand up to shield his eyes from the reflection and tried to peer inside, between the mass of small adverts taped to the inside of the door. There was no welcoming light. It was certainly closed.

Peter took a step back and looked inquisitively at the door. He shook his head and glanced once more at his watch. No, it was definitely 10.15am. What to do? He looked at the array of adverts on the door and mused that, for the youngsters of today, there was no end of possibilities for their parents to spend money on – piano lessons, singing lessons, maths lessons, children's tai-chi, confidence-building for teenagers, kids 'n' pups – the opportunities were plentiful. In fact, he was so caught up in musing over the richness of children's extra-curricular activities (and that of the people who provided them), that he didn't immediately notice the hand-written 'Back in Five Minutes' sign just above the topmost advert.

Peter looked around at what else there was adorning the frontage of his favourite bookshop. There were the two flanking bookshelves of fairly ordinary looking titles, which he'd walked past many times. There was the handwritten invitation to cover muddy walking boots with those plastic wrappers he'd worn on his increasingly frequent visits to Urology and a dispenser of same. There was, higher up above the Inchstar Books sign, a cascading metal sculpture, bearing the Latin motto 'In Libro Veritas.' Peter took it all in, reflecting that he had seldom given the front of the shop his full consideration and he felt as if he was seeing it for the first time, just as it must look to the many tourists who lingered a while in Cromdyke. It was quite a place.

Still, despite its magnificence, his entry was, at least temporarily, barred and he realised he'd have to find a way to pass the *five* minutes. He turned and went to sit on the bench overlooking the pond. It was a grand view. The sun was behind him and the tallness of the stone-built cottages prevented it illuminating the pond directly but the windows of the houses opposite reflected back some of its light. Swans steered imperiously clear of the squabbling mallards and coots clicked for their young. An early Spring zephyr played with his hair. Peter felt calm and his mind started to drift back to the days of his youth, remembering how he had found solace in quiet places, away from the teasing of his 'friends,' and how, despite its challenges, he had occasionally cycled to Cromdyke, all the way from Ripton. Visions of those bike rides became vivid, so much so that he didn't hear Giles' approaching footsteps and was startled when there was a touch on his shoulder.

'Sorry, Peter, didn't mean to make you jump,' said Giles, apologetically, smiling broadly to mitigate any harm.

'No. No,' said Peter. 'I was miles away. Lovely day!'

'Yes, isn't it?' said Giles. 'Shall we let you in?'

Peter smiled his acceptance and mused on Giles' use of 'we.' Perhaps he felt he was speaking on behalf of the owners and employees of Inchstar Books. More likely it was just an affectation and one he used many times during the day. It always rankled with Peter when people used pretentious or clichéd language, especially when, otherwise, they were perfectly likeable souls.

Once inside, Peter walked purposefully across the floor and headed straight upstairs to the first floor. Giles heard him, via the morse-code creaking of the floorboards, wander around first the landing, then the music room and, surprisingly, the children's room too. Within a minute or so, he was back downstairs.

'What're you after today?' enquired Giles helpfully.

'Is Geoff not in yet?' asked Peter without taking the edge of abruptness from his voice.

'No, he'll be in around 11. He texted me. He's been delayed with one of his suppliers.'

'Well, do you know what'll be on the menu today?'

'Can't ever be certain, not with Geoff, but, what day is it? Thursday, isn't it? Likely to be hotpot, I believe. Veggie, of course!'

That last bit he'd added completely unnecessarily Peter thought. Of course, it was vegetarian hotpot – it was the GreenWay Café – what else would they serve?! It was, though, interesting how proprietors of vegetarian cafés and restaurants felt the urge to imitate meat dishes and, very often, substitute the meat part with something meat-like. Why didn't they just go, whole hog, for (as Marcus might say) 'making the vegetable the star of the dish'?

'But you can't be sure?' Peter enquired.

'No,' said Giles, 'I can't be sure. Geoff's a law unto himself but I'm fairly sure he does at least some dishes, on a regular basis. For his regulars, like you.'

Giles smiled. Peter didn't. This wasn't how he'd seen his morning panning out. He'd envisaged arriving when the shop was quite empty – before the hordes arrived – taking his time on the ground floor, with the new releases, before wending his way to the first floor and surreptitiously perusing the menu. After that, he would meander over all three floors in quiet but earnest pursuit of his prey before adjourning to the café for lunch, as was his habit, at 12.15pm. Now there was no chance of anything being ready by 12.15pm AND what exactly would be ready, nobody'd know until 11! All very unsatisfactory.

He looked at his watch. 10.25. Another thirty-five minutes to kill before Geoff would even arrive! What to do? He looked into Giles' bespectacled face but there was no immediate answer in the bland benignity he found there.

'Oh well,' he managed and walked over to the New Releases.

Giles busied himself with sorting out the post into piles, ringing some no doubt important information into the till and switching on the computer they used mostly for searching for books Inchstar might have somewhere in its farthest nooks and crannies, or not at all. With his early morning routine complete, he glanced over at Peter.

'You might be interested in that new one on Continental Tramways, Past and Present,' he suggested. Giles spoke in that way that revealed the capital letters.

Peter weighed the suggestion. He had once told Giles that he volunteered at the local heritage tramway museum, so he could see the logic in Giles' idea. What he had never bothered to tell Giles, or anyone else for that matter, was that he wasn't that interested in trams. He volunteered there, in the summer months, as a way of interacting with people, playing out a role and doing good. The trams, interesting curios though they were, served simply as the backdrop for this. 'Right, OK, thanks,' he said, and looked along the shelf for it.

Now he was obliged to find it, peruse it for an

appropriate amount of time and make some sort of dismissive comment to indicate that he wouldn't be buying it. Oh well. It'd pass the time.

By the time he'd done all of that, he glanced at his watch and saw that it was 10.43 and, just as he was calculating that Geoff would be at least another seventeen minutes, the door opened and in walked Geoff, burdened with a wooden box full of fresh produce. 'Morning, all!' he breezed.

'Morning, both,' thought Peter.

'Sorry I'm late but Whitworths let me down, at the last minute, and I had to trek all the way over to Three Dales, to Johnstone's, to fetch this lot.'

'Still, you're here now,' said Giles and smiled.

Geoff smiled back and strode over towards the stairs but was halted in his tracks by Peter's voice. 'What're you cooking today, then, Geoff?'

Geoff turned. 'Sorry, Peter,' he said, 'didn't see you there. So, yes, today, then, it's going to be moussaka. How does that sound?' He beamed at Peter.

'Fine,' said Peter, managing to inject a scintilla of enthusiasm. 'Yes, that sounds great. Any idea how long?'

'Well, I'm starting late, so I'm afraid it'll be around 1 o'clock. You can't hurry a good moussaka!'

Peter wasn't sure how Geoff knew that to be true. Moussaka had never appeared on the menu before, as far as he could remember, so preparing and baking the moussaka, in the kitchen equipment available upstairs would, necessarily, be a voyage of discovery for Geoff. He was sceptical whether one o'clock would be achieved.

'I won't delay you, then,' said Peter, 'you'll be keen to crack on.'

'Yes, yes, I am,' replied Geoff and turned, somewhat hesitantly back towards the stairs. 'Right, then,' he said and plodded off upstairs, a little unsteadily under the burden of the wooden box.

***

Peter found a quiet spot, on the top floor, in 'Art & Literature.' He picked up a book for appearances' sake, but didn't even glance at the page where he had it open. He stared out of the window, across the pond, and considered moussaka. 'So,' he thought, 'what are the predominant flavours?' In his head, a list began to appear:

'Lamb – the 'Rolls Royce of meats' – sweet;
Aubergine – can be bitter but, if properly prepared… difficult to say – texture more than taste;
Garlic – the queen of ingredients – a sharp onion;
Tomato – sweet;
Cinnamon – sweet;
Béchamel Sauce – creamy.'

'So,' he thought, 'in summary, it's a savoury dish, whose predominant flavours will be sweet but, perhaps, the greater sensation will be texture (with the aubergines and béchamel).' He mused, finally, on what Geoff would be substituting for the lamb. Surely not another vegetable, since that would clash with the aubergine. 'No,' he reasoned, 'it'll doubtless be soybean or something from Linda McCartney.' It definitely needed something, on this occasion, which looked like meat, but, whatever it was, it'd bring no flavour with it. The seasoning would be the thing.

Time to move on. He closed the unattended book, returned it to its space on the shelf and walked out of 'Art & Literature.' Across the landing was 'Biography & Great Lives.' Peter had often mused on what the difference might be between these two labels. Perhaps 'Biography' included lesser lives and, if so, he wondered whose book might be so categorised. Perhaps those still too young to have any achievements of note. Perhaps all those contemporary souls who had been sprung to fame without, actually, having done anything. The blonde-haired motormouths with columns in *The Daily Mail*.

Anyway, once again, he took down a book and opened it at random. He sat in the wing-backed armchair and looked around at the titles. Yes, he'd been right. There was almost an exact 50:50 split between those whose lives he would like to know more about and those whose stories would be the fodder of the Great Unwashed. 'O Brave New World that hath such people in it,' he thought.

Now to setting. He thought back over times when he had eaten moussaka. The holiday in Cyprus, of course. That time, in the '90s when he'd been working in Bulgaria and had to go to Thessaloniki to renew his visa. The Greek restaurant in Ashwater. In truth, he wasn't now quite sure whether he'd had moussaka at all these places – it was often his habit to experiment with new dishes. But still, even if he had eaten moussaka, there was nothing memorable about the location. The one time that stood out was when he and Mary had spent Christmas in Australia with Mary's relatives and had gone to a restaurant in the Greek quarter of Melbourne. 'The Greek Precinct' he remembered it was called, and what a lively place it had been. The restaurant itself had had stalactites descending from the ceiling, though he couldn't now remember its name. Yes, that was a place! The waiters were fantastic (if a little stereotypically Greek), the place had been packed and the other diners were sufficiently buoyed by wine to be willing to join in the singing and dancing. It was quite an evening and he had definitely had moussaka there because Mary's sister-in-law had specifically recommended it. He smacked his lips.

'Hungry?'

The voice startled him. He had been so deep in reverie that he'd completely overlooked the entrance of a young woman into the room. He looked at her, slightly wide-eyed.

'Oh, sorry to have made you jump,' she said, 'it was just that I saw you smacking your lips and I thought, perhaps, that you had missed breakfast. They don't do it here, do they? Only lunches, I think.'

'Yes, that's right,' Peter managed, recovering his composure, 'oh, and afternoon teas.'

'Oh, OK,' said the woman. 'Anyway, I came in here to look for Heather Mills' biography. Do you happen to know where it might be?'

'I'm sorry, I don't,' said Peter but, instead of turning away to look on the shelves, the woman continued to stare at him.

'I'm sorry, I'm afraid I don't know where that book might be.' Peter tried a longer explanation in case the woman hadn't quite caught what he said the first time. She still stared at him and a silence ensued.

'Unless I'm mistaken,' said the woman in a determined voice, 'you're holding it in your hand.'

'What?!' said Peter, instantly flicking the book over to look at its cover and discovering, to his shock and alarm that he was, in fact, holding 'Out on a Limb' with a picture of a young long-legged woman on the front. 'Heather Mills' he read and thought he vaguely recognised her.

'Yes, yes,' he said, flustered. A couple of possible explanations (both lies, obviously) came to mind but he could see where that might lead – having to invent more lies. Lies piled upon lies like a verbal heap of manure. 'No, no,' he thought, 'keep it simple.' He stood, walked over to her and gave her the book. 'Enjoy!' he added, over his shoulder, as he strode past. 'Nice touch,' he thought.

He descended to the first floor and was tempted to go sit in the café but it had always been his habit to avoid the café until dinnertime. Instead, he diverted into 'Hobbies & Home' and found a bench to sit on. He never normally came in here, having previously worked out that it was full of books nobody really wanted. No, his purpose wasn't to look for any books. It was to take stock. He recapped: the flavours were sweet and creamy; the setting was an Australian summer, preferably in Melbourne. Yes, that was it – both criteria covered. A deep intake of breath assured him he was ready. He looked at his watch. 11.15, so he had an hour and three quarters to find what he was looking for. Let the quest begin!

***

In Peter's mind lay heroic intent: he was on a secret mission to which no-one else was, or should be, privy. In Giles' mind, Peter was wandering round the bookshop, much in the same way as he did every Thursday, probably looking for some obscure book or another. In the mind of the young woman, Peter was in denial – he could look as high-brow as he liked; she knew what his real taste in books was. In Geoff's mind, Peter didn't figure at all – Geoff was trying to work out how little time he could leave the salt on the aubergine slices and still ensure that all the bitterness was exorcised. And so Peter roamed over the three floors of Inchstar Books, completely misunderstood or neglected by all his witnesses. He liked it that way.

Peter knew that the non-fiction sections were very unlikely to be fertile territory but, nonetheless and for the sake of completeness, he swept down Inchstar Books from the top floor to the ground. Along the way, he did, occasionally, stop and consider a book but, if he was honest, these were not candidates for this week's Grail. They were books that took his interest in other directions and represented that perpetual joy of bookshops – real browsing. The ground floor was where fiction was and, in his gut, he knew that this week's choice had to be fiction.

***

Peter arrived in the café at 12.50, book in hand. As soon as he began negotiating his way past the movable door, which swung heavily, bedecked with shelving on both sides, through the arc determined by the metal channels set into floor and ceiling, the smell hit him. Aromas of cinnamon and garlic fired the synapses which meant Australia and laughter and food. Yes, he was in the right place and, in his hand, was just the right book.

'It'll be another ten minutes yet,' called Geoff from the galley behind the counter. 'Can I get you a drink?'

'Just a glass of tap water will be fine,' said Peter.

'Coming up.'

Peter found a seat amongst the cluttered collection of wooden tables and chairs but, then, almost immediately rose again as Geoff slid a glass of water onto the counter. 'Thanks, Geoff,' he said with a tad more zeal that a glass of water warranted. He sat back down, facing the whole (but empty) café and opened his book. He sat forward so that he could keep the cover close to the table top and flattened the pages with a respectful pressure. He began reading.

By the time Geoff shouted, 'Ready!' Peter was in that pleasant phase where his mind swam entirely within the sea of the story. He had grasped and was starting to know some of the characters and, more importantly, was 'living' in a Perth suburb. He was immersed in the world of the book in that way that only reading can provide. Geoff's voice punctured his pleasure and, had it not been for the imminence of the food, he would have reacted more sourly. 'OK,' he said brightly.

Peter allowed the moussaka to stand steaming for five minutes, partly because he didn't like his food red hot and partly because the novel was starting to grip him. He reached the end of Chapter One and resurfaced to contemplate his food. Geoff had provided a generous portion, splayed on the plate in an untidy oblong with slices of aubergine protruding here and there, béchamel oozing and garlic vying with oregano and nutmeg to entice his nose. Lentils were the visible substitute for meat. Brown lentils, possibly Puy.

'How is it?' enquired Geoff from behind the counter.

'Well, if look and smell are anything to go by, it'll taste great but I haven't tasted it just yet. Can I ask, though, are these Puy lentils?'

'They are,' said Geoff proudly, 'I wanted to include the best.'

'Great!' said Peter and brought a forkful to his mouth. 'Mmm, very nice,' was his verdict, although, in truth, it was still a fraction too hot to fully savour. 'I'll let you know my verdict when I've finished.' Peter was anxious to get back to his book and he knew, from past experience, that, if you let Geoff get started, he could rattle on no end. He looked pointedly at his book and allowed the fork to hover. Geoff took the hint but made rather a lot of noise washing up the pots and pans.

Chapter Two was the onset of the drama in the book and Peter knew that it wouldn't be sweet – it never was – but hoped for interludes. It was always around this point that he started to wonder whether he'd made the right choice. Today, he'd given initial consideration to 'Chocolat' for its obvious pleasantness and to some of the classics of Australian literature ('Thorn Birds,' 'Oscar and Lucinda,' 'Picnic at Hanging Rock') but none he thought would quite deliver what he was after. He'd settled for this and he'd have to see it through.

He read on.

The moussaka disappeared, forkful by forkful, sometimes attended for flavour, sometimes not, as the characters and drama deepened their grip on Peter. When he noticed he'd just eaten but not thought about it, he reproached himself but reasoned that, perhaps, the book was simply too good for simultaneous thinking. Nonetheless, that was what he was here for. 'Must try harder,' he resolved. He organised his next forkful to include all the ingredients and placed it carefully onto his tongue. He noticed the overlap of the sharp garlic with the smooth aubergine and appreciated the accents brought by the herbs and spices. In order to hold onto the flavour, as he dipped back into the book, he smacked his lips.

'Well, you can't still be hungry!'

The voice shot across the café, across the table, across his book and buried itself smack in the middle of his consciousness. He looked up but, even as he did so, he knew exactly whose voice it was. 'No,' he said. He knew that politeness dictated more but he had been ejected forcibly from the very essence of what he was here to do and he resented it. He looked at her.

She smiled. 'Remember me?' she said and he couldn't tell if it was slightly sarcastic. 'Heather Mills' biography?' He nodded, still in the grip of resentment. She smiled again and Peter could tell that she wasn't for giving up. He dredged up all the protocol he could. 'Yes, of course,' he said.

'How's the food? Moussaka, is it? Smells delicious.'

'Yes,' said Peter, 'it's good.'

She looked at him to see if he was going to offer any more but it seemed unlikely. She turned her attention to the menu. 'Hmm,' she mused aloud. 'Moussaka or quiche? – the agony of choice.' Geoff looked at her and raised his eyebrows. 'I think it'll have to be the moussaka, please, since it comes with such a glowing recommendation.'

'Coming up,' said Geoff breezily.

She moved over in Peter's direction. 'Mind if I join you?' she asked.

Peter summoned up all his charm. 'No.' A pause. 'No, not at all.' She sat down at a closely adjacent table, clearly oblivious to the messages Peter was trying to convey.

'It's a lovely shop, isn't it? I've never been here before – never been to Cromdyke, even. It's really lovely round here.' She looked at Peter but, detecting no desire to respond, ploughed on: 'but this shop is fantastic. How long's it been here? Looks like it's been here forever.'

'Not really,' said Peter, 'mid-seventies.'

'Oh,' said the woman. She looked at Peter. The clock

behind the counter ticked. Peter looked at the woman.

'Moussaka!' announced Geoff and placed a plate on the counter.

'Thank you,' said the woman and, calculating that it would be down to her to fetch it, got up and retrieved it, along with a knife, fork and serviette. She sat back down. 'Looks lovely,' she said to no-one in particular. No-one responded. For the next few moments the woman was quiet and Peter started to hope that she would abate and he'd be able to get back to his book.

'What're you reading?' she tried.

Peter knew that he would be obliged to reveal his book but, even as he started to raise it to show her, doubted whether it would be of any interest. After all, she was someone who read the biographies of minor celebrities, someone who probably hadn't dabbled in literature since she'd been obliged to at school, someone with whom he wouldn't have very much in common.

Suspecting that she would feel obliged to ask some inane question about it, he started to formulate a response, based on an outline of the story, the setting and the main characters. Maybe he wouldn't even need to talk about the characters. She looked like the sort of woman who wasn't interested unless the people were well-known and stereotyped. No, he'd be fine to tell her what the story was about. If he said 'Australia,' she'd probably fill in the rest from her doubtless extensive knowledge of life down under. He raised the cover to show her.

'Oh,' she said, '*Cloudstreet*. A great book. I think you'll love it.'

After Hours

Don turned the key twice in the front door and paused to look around the frontage of the Spice Islands Café. Nothing had been left out – the tables and chairs were carefully stored inside, the fruit and veg had been returned to cold storage and the wicker baskets had been re-stacked on the shelves. Belster wasn't a particularly high-crime area but it was always as well to check everything, one last time, before leaving for the night. He was satisfied that all was as it should be, and that calm had been restored. He turned and walked away.

Inside, sounds were few. There was an occasional click as a motion sensor checked itself for alertness. There was a low hum of contentment, from the glass-fronted fridges, as 2°C was maintained. There was the creaking of wicker as the various baskets, hampers and trugs settled into a comfortable arrangement with gravity. Otherwise, there was nothing. Nothing, that is, except the aftermath of a day's trading with customers who had entered the café with expectations and left with those expectations either satisfied, surpassed or dashed. The accompanying feelings were all around and the air was pregnant with potential.

Surprisingly, first to show itself was a scintilla of smugness. It dawned upon the area just in front of the counter, glowed and then faded. It was a rich purple in hue and took on the shape of a shawl. This was the imprint of April Parkinson, whose elevated discussion with her friend on the mezzanine had interrupted the conversations at all the other tables. 'Was it latte or cappuccino? I can never remember which one you have.' Her friend mouthed 'latte' down to her but April hadn't finished yet. 'Oh, yes, that's the one without the sprinkles, isn't it?' Her friend nodded. The embarrassed irritation now shone brown and oblong like a smear. It would re-appear several times that night.

In the kitchen, just behind the open semi-circle which was the hatch, a sharp jag of sound rent the air but for a fraction of a second and no more. Nor was its volume high. It erupted and was gone so fast no human witness would be quite certain that it had happened at all. This was the disbelieving shock of Lottie Kirk, head cook. The grey-handled knife whose perpetual sharpness she insisted upon had bitten her, slicing through the flesh and nail of her left index finger, as it whirled in the rhythmic oscillations carefully honed at catering college. The irony was not lost on Bev, the owner, whose frequent admonishments to 'be careful' were, she often felt, lost on Lottie's impetuous youth.

Behind the counter, the unmistakeable tang of garlic sprang out. Missing from the delivery and requiring three phone calls to try to rectify, the absence of garlic had tormented Ryan, the assistant manager. Ryan had paced up and down, increasingly fearful that the garlic wouldn't be sourceable that day and they'd either have to make something not involving garlic (Heaven forbid!) or they'd have to open a jar of garlic puree. Ryan loved garlic – considerably more than his girlfriend – and a day without it, he thought, threatened the reputation of the Spice Islands Café. In the end, they had managed with asafoetida, a type of giant fennel, which Lottie had said would give a similar flavour. She was wrong and the smell, before cooking, was horrendous. Finally now, here was that garlic incense once more, just as Ryan had wished and, all the more powerful for it.

All manifestations were suspended, though, as the latch clicked and the front door opened. In crept Lottie and her boyfriend, Charlie. Lottie had been entrusted with a key, one day last week, when she'd volunteered to be there to open the shop for an early delivery of craft pies. She'd 'forgotten' to give the key back to Bev and was now making use of it, in a way that Bev neither knew about nor would have approved of. 'Still, what care I?' thought Lottie. Once they were both inside, Lottie turned and re-locked the door. She glanced, through the shop window, up and down the street. Nobody.

Charlie whispered, 'So what now?'

'Find somewhere to sit and just wait.'

Charlie took a seat on one of the metal stools around the main bench table in the middle of the room.

'No, not there, obvs!' said Lottie. 'Not in view of the window. Anyone could see you there.'

Charlie got up and moved to a table in the corner. 'This OK?' he queried sarcastically.

Lottie nodded, gave him a reproving look to anchor him in his new position, and went off round to the kitchen. Charlie saw her head appear, through the hatch, but couldn't work out what she might be doing. He realised, then, that only limited planning had gone into this venture and the words of his old TA sergeant came to mind: 'Failing to plan is planning to fail.' He'd been bowled along by Lottie's enthusiasm without considering the fact that they were now actually committing a crime. 'What're you doing?' he sent a stage whisper in Lottie's direction.

'Shh.' She went on doing whatever it was, for a few moments longer, before disappearing from view again. She reappeared to his left, having exited the kitchen via a different door, and it made him jump slightly.

'What've you been doing?' he asked.

'Just setting everything up. It's done now,' she said and sat down alongside Charlie, both facing into the café. 'Right, then,' she said. 'Silence.'

Charlie looked at her and, in the streetlight coming through the shop window, could see her seriousness and determination. He'd known her long enough to read the signals, although he was getting ever more anxious about their situation. Torn between wanting to speak and wanting to leave, he shifted slightly in his chair. Lottie favoured him with a look and he exhaled, resigned to some period of inactivity.

They both looked into the body of the café, Lottie sweeping her gaze over the all-too-familiar territory and Charlie looking at the chilled counters and imagining the pies and pastries that usually occupied those spaces. Eventually they found themselves both focusing on the piles of wicker on the shelves to the side of the counter. Lottie had heard creaks from there before and Charlie was thinking about what he'd put into his ideal hamper, mentally stocking it with huntsman's pie, pickles, and cupcakes.

'I can almost taste them,' said Charlie, smacking his lips together.

'Almost taste what?' said Lottie, exasperation in her voice.

'Those huntsman's pies. The ones they sell here, with that apple sauce topping.'

'What're you talking about? Almost taste them? If there's any left, and I don't think there are – I think we sold the last of them this afternoon – but, if there are, by chance, any left, they'll all be safely tucked away in the fridge out back.'

'I'm telling you I can taste them… well, almost taste them. No, I think I can actually taste them. The ham, the turkey and the apple sauce. I can definitely taste them.'

'Yeah, yeah,' said Lottie.

'Here, then. Try this.' And, with that, he swooped in

on her, kissed her full on the lips and began exploring her mouth with his tongue.

At first, she resisted, torn between the effrontery of the gesture but then warming to the spontaneity and passion. His tongue was everywhere, like an electric eel in her mouth and, initially, it was all sensation of touch but, then, something started to happen. The distinctive sharpness of apple became a clear note in her mouth, followed by the saltiness of ham and was there also the aftertaste of turkey?' This was distinctly odd – Lottie was not a fan of the pies, yet she could clearly taste them now on Charlie's breath and tongue. Where had that come from?

'See?' said Charlie, as he broke off.

'Hmm,' was all Lottie could manage, her mind whirling with explanations as to how those flavours came to be apparent in the mouth of someone not eating anything.

They sat in silence for a few moments before Charlie said: 'I can't believe that. The taste's gone now but it was just as if I was eating a pie.'

'Hmm,' said Lottie, but offered nothing more. This would need thinking about but that could come later. 'Let's just be quiet and see what else happens,' she said, eventually.

'OK,' said Charlie, 'but odd.'

They sat there in silence, once more, conscious of the machinery working to maintain the operation of the café but trying hard to be conscious of what might lie above and beyond that. Minutes went by with both of them straining every ounce of concentration into perception. If anything else transpired, they were both now determined not to miss it.

'What?' asked Charlie, suddenly.

'Shh,' said Lottie.

'You just touched me on the arm.'

'No, I didn't.'

'Well, somebody did. I felt it.'

'Well, it wasn't me,' said Lottie definitively.

Shaggy's lyrics came instantly to Charlie's mind but he realised that this might not be the right time for making musical references. 'Someone definitely just brushed my arm,' he said.

Lottie turned her head and looked at him closely but could see, even in the orange streetlight, that he was serious. He was holding his forearm and stroking it gently with his fingertips. 'Just like this,' he said, gesturing.

'Well, that's strange,' she said. 'Are you sure it was a definite touch? Not just your shirt sleeve flopping down?'

'My shirt sleeve's rolled up and has been since we've been here. All night, actually. So, no, it wasn't my shirt sleeve or anything else. It was a touch on the arm, as if someone was trying to get my attention.'

'Curiouser and curiouser,' said Lottie. 'Keep still and see if it happens again.' Charlie nodded and, once more, faced the café, mentally daring whatever was there to touch him again. Lottie hoped something would and, keeping her head perfectly still, looked sidelong at everything within her field of vision. Nothing moved, nor made a sound. They were both breathing in the top of their lungs, as if to take a deep breath would break the spell. Lottie thought that she had never paid closer attention to her senses, nor felt more alive, than she did in that moment.

And in was exactly in that moment that the door suddenly swung open and the shop lights all came on, at the same time. Lottie and Charlie jumped in their chairs, but this was far from the supernatural experience they had been hoping for. It was Bev and Don and they weren't happy.

'What on earth are you doing here?' Bev demanded, looking hard at Lottie but taking occasional glances at Charlie.

Lottie blinked in the harsh light and shielded her eyes. 'Look, erm, Mrs Spicer, we're sorry. We were just…' said Charlie but, before he could continue, Bev cut sharply across his words.

'I was asking Lottie!' she announced.

'We were just…' said Lottie, 'investigating whether the café was haunted.'

'Haunted?!' said Bev. 'Haunted?! How could the café be haunted?! Nobody's died here. At least, not to my knowledge. Don, have you heard of anyone dying here?' Don shook his head and looked sternly at Lottie. Bev, too, stared at Lottie.

'But, just as important, how did you get in here?'

'With the key you gave me, when I came in early to take that delivery from Jackman's. Remember? You had a hospital appointment, I think.'

'Yes, yes, I remember. But why didn't you return the

34

key to me, afterwards? There's no way you should be holding on to a key for this place.'

'You didn't ask me and, I suppose, it just slipped my mind.'

'Well, either that, or you saw a way of creeping back in here, after dark, to have some sort of 'party' with your boyfriend here.' She looked searchingly at Charlie and then at Lottie.

'No, it wasn't like that at all,' said Lottie, as if suddenly realising quite how things might look. 'We were just investigating. Look over there if you don't believe me.' She pointed over to the hatch where a camera was sitting on a mini-tripod and a recording device of some sort was facing out into the café. Don walked over to them, picked each up in turn and examined them. 'I've no idea what these are,' he said.

'That one's an infra-red camera,' said Lottie, nodding towards the camera, 'for recording heat signatures and the other one's an EVP recorder.'

'EVP?' said Don

'Electronic Voice Phenomena,' said Lottie. 'The camera helps us see unexplained phenomena and the EVP helps us hear them.'

Don looked dubiously at them again and then back over at Bev. He shrugged. 'Seems plausible,' he said. There was a pause in the discussions as no-one was sure what to say or do next.

'Well, anyway,' said Bev, 'there's no way in the world that you should be doing this without our permission. I'm going to need to discuss this with Don and we'll let you know tomorrow what we've decided. Please collect up your things and go. Oh, and I'll have that key back now.'

Lottie and Charlie did as they were asked and hurried out of the café. 'Sorry, sorry,' said Lottie, as they left, but there was no reply.

***

Two days later and Charlie and Lottie were sitting at the table in her flat.

'So what've you been doing with yourself?' asked Charlie.

'Much the same as you, I expect,' said Lottie, 'enjoying my hopefully temporary disconnection from the wonderful world of work.'

'You'll get something soon,' said Charlie, 'people always have to eat.'

'Yes,' said Lottie, 'I know but it was good working there. It was a big happy family and, now I feel like a bit of an outcast. Over one stupid mistake, too!'

'Yes well, no use crying over spilt milk. It's done now and you'll just have to move on,' said Charlie. 'I still don't know how they found out, though.'

'Motion sensors,' said Lottie. 'I completely forgot about them and they send a message straight to the owners. Really, in some ways, we were lucky it didn't go through to the police station. I wouldn't have fancied trying to explain what we were up to, to some coppers with tasers. And neither would you!' She looked directly at Charlie.

'No,' he said, looking down.

A moment passed as they contemplated that particular scene and others from their pasts.

'Anyway,' said Charlie, 'let's have a look at the footage and see if anything materialised. I was sure somebody touched me and there was that funny incident with the taste in my mouth. That was odd.'

'I've already listened to the EVP and there's nothing on there,' said Lottie, 'but I haven't had chance to look through the video. Let's do that.'

Charlie picked up the camera and, plugged it straight into Lottie's laptop. He angled it so that they both could see clearly, and set it running. They watched the screen, anxious to detect any detail of colour variation in the scene.

'You look hot,' said Lottie, pointing to the unmistakeable white colour of Charlie's forehead on the screen.

'Well, I was sitting next to you,' said Charlie, and glanced at her. Lottie kept looking at the screen.

They watched in silence, seeing nothing change but noting the interesting colours of the scene and mentally remarking how the busy places – the door, the floor and the seating – continued to hold onto some heat, long after they had been used.

'How long were we there?' asked Charlie, eventually.

'Keep looking,' said Lottie, 'we don't want to miss anything. And, anyway, I should have thought you'd want to see some real evidence, since it was you who said they'd experienced something.'

'Yeah, OK,' said Charlie and renewed his attention.

They watched attentively but saw nothing unusual, apart from the moment where they had kissed and both noticed how Lottie's normal array of greens and blues had suddenly shot up through the colours and was, by the end, almost entirely red and white.

'Hmm,' said Charlie but Lottie ignored him.

Finally, all the lights came on, in the video, and they sat back in their chairs and looked at each other.

'Disappointing,' said Charlie.

'Yes,' said Lottie, got up and walked towards the kitchen. 'Coffee?' she asked over her shoulder. There was silence and Lottie turned to look at Charlie. He was staring very closely at the screen.

'Never mind that,' he said, 'does the camera always shoot in infra-red?'

'No, not always,' said Lottie, walking back over to the table. 'When there's sufficient natural or artificial light, it films on normal wavelengths. Why?'

'Look at this,' he said and pointed to the images in the doorway.

Around the smaller of the two figures entering, now clearly visible as Bev, was an intermittent but clear flash of red.

'See that?!' Charlie almost shouted.

'Yes, yes. Crikey. Yes. That's not a heat signature; that's something else. Blimey. Wonder what that is.' She turned to look at Charlie but his gaze was still locked to the screen.

'Yes, but that's not the most interesting. Look at

this!' he said pointed to the other figure. Completely surrounding Don was a shimmering pulsating aura, like a cloak of protection.

It was black.

Less is More

Above and behind the counter was a large chalkboard menu, with three panels. On the centre one was written the following:

We serve a Standard Breakfast.
It includes:
2 x Bacon
1 x Egg
2 x Sausage
Beans
Mushrooms
1 x Toast

It costs £5.25 (including tea or coffee)

We do not alter this menu.
However, the customer is always right and

you may wish to add or subtract items.
Any change whatsoever incurs a charge of 50p.

'Have you seen that?' I said, pointing.

Becky stood for a moment, reading.

'Sounds like the guy who runs this place takes no prisoners,' she said. She looked round at the other notices, of which there were quite a few. I followed her eyes.

'No muddy boots past this point. No exceptions'
'If you want to keep the newspaper, buy it. It costs £5'
'If you take your tray outside, bring it back in'
'No dogs except for the blind'
'Toilet for customers only. Minimum spend £5'

'Yes,' I said and peered through the hatch into the kitchen to see if I could spot the man with the no-nonsense manner. There was plenty of activity there but the height of the hatch didn't allow a view of any faces, so quite which one Mr Grumpy was, remained in doubt. It certainly wasn't the lad serving on at the counter, who greeted each customer with a smile and a 'What can I get you?'

Despite the hour, the cafe was already busy. Most of the visible tables seemed occupied and several of the outside ones, too. The queue, with about half a dozen folk already in it, snaked round the room. Becky and I smiled at one another and joined it. We were always up for a new experience.

As people were dealt with, the queue edged forward

until it was the turn of the couple in front of us. They looked as if they were in their thirties and wore matching anoraks. It was at this point that Mr Grumpy arrived – if it wasn't Mr Grumpy himself, it was certainly his understudy – and stood beside the lad at the counter. He nodded towards the till and the lad seemed to understand something by that. They both turned towards the couple at the counter.

'What can I get you?' asked the lad serving.

'Can I get two breakfasts, please? One with tea, one with coffee?' said the man.

'You can *have* two breakfasts,' said Mr Grumpy flatly.

'Sorry?' said the man.

'You can *have* two breakfasts. You can't *get* two breakfasts cos that's our job. We do the getting.'

'Oh,' said the man. 'In that case, can I *have* two breakfasts?'

'Please,' said Mr Grumpy. He and the man locked stares. 'Good manners cost nothing.'

'He said *please*' said the woman. 'Before, when he asked at first. Before you started with the business about *get* and *have*.'

'Yes, I did,' chimed the man, suddenly emboldened. They were united now in confrontation and green attire. The café, at least the interior of the café, had quieted, as conversations were quelled in favour of listening to the exchange. This is what they had come for.

'Right,' said Mr Grumpy, finally. 'Is that it? Two breakfasts, then. Give 'em a ticket, Liam. That'll be £10.50.'

The opportunity hung in the air for the woman to demand a *please* in return but, even as she was considering it, the man spoke. 'One without beans, please,' he said, cutting away the ground from under her. They seemed, just in that moment, curiously disunited, and Mr Grumpy seized the moment.

'That'll be £11.00, please, then,' he said.

'What!?' said the woman.

'£11.00,' said Mr Grumpy, '£5.25 for the Standard Breakfast, times two, plus 50p for the change on one of them.' He pointed towards the writing on the chalkboard.

'But we're *not* having something,' said the woman, the indignation proud in her voice.

'Yes, that's right,' said Mr Grumpy. 'You're making one change to the menu and we're charging you for that change, as clearly advertised here on the menu.' He tapped the chalkboard.

'But we're *not* having one item. We're not asking for something instead. We're just doing without one portion of beans.'

'Yes,' said Mr Grumpy, 'and that's a change, is it not?'

'Let me get this straight…' The woman's voice had now moved up a notch on the indignation scale and, with it, an octave in pitch. 'You want to charge us for having nothing!'

'As clearly stated.' Mr Grumpy tapped the board again. 'So, do you want the breakfasts, or don't you? We've got quite a long queue of people waiting,' and gestured towards the rest of us.

'I think you might be able to guess the answer to that

question,' said the woman. Mr Grumpy returned her gaze with complete indifference. 'Come on, John.'

She favoured Mr Grumpy with one last volcanic stare, turned, and walked towards the door. The café held its breath to see if there might be a parting shot, at the doorway, but none came. Even as they strode away from the door, nothing was said. Eruption forestalled.

There was a pause before the conversations in the café started up again, quickly shifting from low murmurings to joyous reflections. Becky and I stood, for a moment, where we were, still absorbing the events which had just played out right in front of us. Then, as if emerging from a deep dive, I surfaced back into the world of hazardous interaction and took a step forward.

'What can I get you?' asked the lad serving.

'Well…' I began.

Café@Lizzie's

Betty walked across, from the kitchen door, to where the tray trolley stood, parked against the wall. This took a little time as Betty's knees weren't what they were and, just lately, her hip had been giving her some gyp, too. But she put a brave face on it all and smiled at a group of nurses who were sat at one of the tables. One of them smiled back and watched Betty walk over to the trolley. It was as tall as Betty and laden, on the top few rungs, with trays of the usual detritus of café life: cups, plates, cutlery and crisp packets – they were always crisp packets.

Betty pulled the trolley out from its place, causing it to squeal as a faulty castor complained. She surveyed the collection of items and distributed them so that all the rubbish was on one tray. She slid that one out and turned in the direction of the bins. As she did so, a crisp packet wafted off the tray and floated past Betty's hand to the floor. Betty looked down at it and the nurse who'd been watching her jumped up and retrieved it.

'Oh, thank you, love,' said Betty and smiled, all white teeth and crow's feet. The nurse smiled back, all lip gloss and eyeliner.

Betty took the tray of rubbish over to the bins. She dutifully recycled what could be recycled and put the rest into the bin marked 'landfill.' She tapped the top of the green recycle bin and walked back over to the trolley, once more.

Before starting on her rounds, Betty looked across the café. Since its refurbishment, last year, and its rebranding 'Café@Lizzie's,' it had become quite the hub of the whole hospital. The seating, which varied from the ubiquitous plastic-and-metal chairs to some padded benches to a few high-backed plastic-covered armchairs, was about half full. She looked at the clock. 8.45. Yes, that was about right for this time of day. Several of the tables, set out in approximate rows, were occupied by solitary middle-aged or elderly men. It was Thursday – Urology day. At the table nearest to her, though, sat a couple – in their fifties or sixties, Betty estimated – and the man had his arm gently across the back of the woman. They were leaning in towards one another and the woman was cradling a beaker of coffee. Her first port of call.

The trolley with its wonky castor had a mind of its own, sometimes, Betty knew that, but she coaxed it towards the couple and, for once, it didn't put up any resistance. As she approached the table, she could begin to discern a few words from their conversation: '… don't know…'; ' too young… '; 'Doctor Bradshaw said…' So that she didn't startle them, Betty brought the trolley round in a wide sweep to face them.

'Can I just clear away the empties?' she said breezily, smiling gently but genuinely.

'Yes, yes, of course,' said the man, sitting back. Betty came to the table edge and assembled the items on the tray in close formation. She pulled the tray towards her, all the time looking at the bowed head of the woman. Sensing this, the woman sat back, too, still cradling her coffee and looked up into Betty's eyes. For a second, nothing was said.

'Lovely day,' said the woman. The man looked at her and frowned, clearly surprised at the comment.

'Yes, isn't it,' said Betty, 'and perhaps a bit of sunshine later.'

'That'll be nice,' said the woman.

The man looked from the woman to Betty and back again. He smiled faintly and looked again at then both in sequence. Neither spoke.

'Thank you,' said the woman and then, as if remembering something, pushed her beaker across to Betty.

'That's fine, love,' said Betty, smiled warmly at both, and picked up the beaker and put it on the tray. She picked up the tray and slid it effortlessly onto one of the rungs and pushed the trolley away. As she walked, she again caught snippets of their whispered conversation: '… kind… , '…see him soon…, '…better…'

The next table she approached had a single elderly man sitting at it. He was reading a newspaper but, as she drew nearer, she saw that his hands were trembling. In front of him was a small beaker of coffee, now empty.

'Would you like another one of those?' asked Betty and the man looked up. His eyes were watery and wide and the irises slightly indistinct at the edges, as if they had bled into the whites. He stared at Betty, uncomprehending. 'Another coffee?' Betty helped out.

'Oh, no, love, thank you,' he said. 'I'm afraid I can only afford one, here, at these prices.'

'But they have an offer on, now, so if you buy one coffee, you can have a second one free.' Betty smiled and the man felt instantly re-assured and relieved.

'Oh, then, that would be lovely,' he said, 'it's just black,' and offered up his cup. Betty took it and walked over to the automated coffee machine, dispensing all shades of coffee and two shades of hot chocolate, too. She put his cup under the array of nozzles, pressed 'Black' and waited whilst it whirred, gurgled and expressed a cup's worth of coffee. She picked it up and walked round the corner, past the till, where Rose was standing. As she walked past, Betty winked at Rose and pushed two coins across the counter. Rose smiled.

'There you are, love,' said Betty, when she got back to his table, 'courtesy of St Elizabeth.' She placed the cup down in front of him.

'Thank you,' said the man, 'that's lovely. Have they been doing this long?' He nodded towards the coffee. 'I didn't see any signs.'

'Ah, well,' said Betty, but offered no further information. A resigned look, a tilting of her head slightly to the left and that bountiful smile was all she offered and, for the man, that was enough. His inquisitiveness vanished instantly.

He looked down at his cup, hesitated, and then reached towards it with both hands simultaneously. As he did so, he noticed his hands had stopped trembling and he withdrew his left hand, taking the coffee up in his right. He raised an eyebrow, looked into the cup and took a sip. It was delicious!

'Thank you,' he offered. 'That's the best cup of coffee I've had in ages!' He smiled broadly, looking into Betty's gentle gaze. 'I'm glad,' she said.

The group of businessmen at the next table were too engrossed in marketingspeak to pay any attention to Betty and her table-clearing activities. They neither broke off their conversation nor moved unduly, as Betty worked around them to retrieve the crockery and waste. Betty looked from one face to the next but saw no sign of anything except complete engagement with the discussion, almost as if their interactions held them in a sphere above the normal world. They didn't even pause when the wonky wheel squealed rather loudly. As she walked away, she heard the youngest of them say: 'If we could only push the per-unit yield by upselling on a one-in-five basis, the year-end could well be north of ten mill.' Truly lost souls.

Several now-empty tables bore witness to the consumption of a variety of foodstuffs. There were plates besmirched with bean juice – they had held the Standard English Breakfast. There were plates touched with a smear of grease – they had held the Special Blueberry Pancakes with Maple Syrup. There were bowls speckled with oats – they had contained the Scottish Porridge. There were side plates, unsullied, but needing nonetheless to be collected and washed, which had held only fruit and kitkats. And, of course, there were beakers. Betty dutifully rounded them all up.

The table in the far corner was occupied by a solitary woman with grey hair, glasses and her coat buttoned up to the neck. Her hands were underneath the table, clasped in her lap. In front of her were two untouched poached eggs on toast and a glass of water. She was looking round at the folk on adjacent tables but her eyes kept returning to the main doors, as she studied every entrant.

'Not feeling so hungry, today, love?' asked Betty.

The woman shot her a look but, almost immediately, switched it to a half-smile. 'No… well, yes, I suppose I've got to eat something and they said that eggs were a good thing… but I just can't face them.'

'They look like they've gone a bit cold, too,' said Betty. 'Shall I see if I can't get Cook to reheat them for you?'

'Oh, would you?' said the woman. 'That'd be good.'

Betty parked her trolley a little way away, came back and picked up the plate, smiled, and went off to the kitchen. Within moments, she was back and the woman could see the eggs were piping hot.

'I got Cook to do you some fresh toast, too,' said Betty, '… to spruce it up a bit.'

'Thank you so much,' said the woman and lifted her knife and fork. She cut into the first egg and its yolk spilt over the toast. She cut off a corner and lifted it to her mouth. She chewed, a first a little gingerly, but with growing enthusiasm. 'Maybe a bit of salt and pepper?' asked Betty.

'I'm not supposed to 'ave too much salt,' said the woman.

'Just pepper, then?' suggested Betty.

The woman nodded and sprinkled a little from the pot over her food. 'Mmmm,' she said, 'that's good!'

'Are you here alone?' asked Betty.

'No. No, my daughter's coming. She's just parking the car. She dropped me off by the main entrance, cos of my hip. She'll be in, in a minute.'

'I see,' said Betty. 'I'll let you finish your breakfast, then.'

'Oh no, don't feel you have to go away,' said the woman. 'Please, have a seat.'

'Oh, OK then, if you're sure,' said Betty and sat down.

For a moment Betty didn't speak as the woman savoured her breakfast but then ventured: 'Have you come far?'

'No, not really. Well, just from Langwith. Do you know it?'

'Oh yes,' said Betty. 'It's in a lovely spot. Have you lived there long?'

'All my life, really, well, from getting married, that is. I come from Colley originally. Me 'usband's from Langwith. Dave. Oh, I'm being very rude, I 'aven't introduced myself. Kath.' She offered her hand to Betty, who clasped it warmly.

'Betty,' said Betty.

'Yes, I saw,' said Kath, 'on the badge.' She nodded towards the lanyard round Betty's neck. Beneath the crest and the words 'St Elizabeth's Hospital,' she could see Betty's name.

'Oh, I'll take it off just while I'm talking to you,' said Betty, extricating her head from the lanyard and placing the badge on the table. 'And have you got any other children, then, besides your daughter?'

'Yes, another daughter,' said Kath and she leant forward conspiratorially to almost whisper, 'but she lives down South. And a son, Simon.'

'And where does he live?'

'Oh, here, in Rotherley.' Again the conspiratorial lean. 'But he's gay.'

'Oh, that's not such a thing, though, these days, is it?' said Betty.

'No, you do hear more of them about,' agreed Kath, 'but still I worry about AIDS and such. 'E was such a lovely little boy, as well, never a moment's bother. Always clean and tidy. 'E'd do anything for you. So kind and thoughtful. Always remembered my birthday – everyone's birthdays really – right from an early age.'

She paused, as if reflecting on what she had just said. 'Maybe I should have seen it coming... and done something about it.'

'Oh, I don't think there's anything to be done about it,' said Betty, 'gay people are gay and straight people are straight and others are in between. We're all who we are and that's that.' She paused. 'If you see what I mean.'

'Yes, I suppose you're right,' said Kath. 'Can't help worrying, though.'

Kath's eyes were suddenly elsewhere and Betty followed her stare to see a young woman striding across the café in their direction. The woman glanced at Betty but spoke to Kath. 'There, got it done... eventually. Had to park in the furthest car park away and then I had to queue to get in.'

'Yes,' said Betty, 'sometimes this place can be hell.' The young woman looked at Betty and tried to smile.

'Oh, sorry,' said Kath. 'Sarah, this is Betty. Betty, this is Sarah, my daughter.'

'Hello, Sarah,' said Betty and smiled. Sarah found herself smiling back, fulsomely. 'Hello.'

Sarah turned back to her mother. 'So, have you had some breakfast, then? What did you have? Have you drunk enough liquids? It can be quite draining, by all accounts. I'll get you some bottles.' And with that, she stood back up and left the table in the direction of the shop.

'She's quite the whirlwind,' said Kath, 'when she gets the bit between 'er teeth. But a lovely girl. Always there when you need 'er. She's taken the morning off to come with me. And she's got a very demanding job. In HR. Course, her 'usband helps out, Jonathan, with the kids and that.'

'So, you've got grandchildren?' asked Betty.

'Two, so far. A boy and a girl. Six and four. I babysit

regular on a Saturday, so as Sarah and Jonathan can get a bit of time to themselves. They sleep at ours, sometimes, but that's a bit of a squeeze and…' again the conspiratorial lean, 'if I'm honest, they tire me out. Don't say anything to Sarah, mind.'

Betty's smile and slight shake of the head assured Kath of her trustworthy silence on such matters.

'So what are you in for, today?' asked Betty.

'Chemo,' said Kath abruptly.

'And are you worried about it?'

'Terrified, if I'm honest,' said Kath. 'I've read the leaflet they sent, two or three times, but you can't 'elp but think they don't tell you everything. They'd leave out the bad bits, wouldn't they?'

'Oh, I think, they try, nowadays, to prepare you as best they can. Partly, it's because that's the right thing to do and partly because they're scared of getting sued. If they haven't told you something, it's because it's not going to happen.' Betty's gaze and smile spoke to her sincerity and Kath saw this.

'Oh, that's good to know,' said Kath, and suddenly, her tone was lighter.

'What is?' asked Sarah, returning with three half-litre bottles of water.

'Oh, nothing,' said Kath. Sarah looked from her mother to Betty and back again but sensed there was nothing more to come. 'Anyway, I got you Buxley Spring. That's the best, I think.' She looked at Betty for confirmation.

'Yes, I'm sure it's very good. Seems very popular.'

There was a momentary pause in conversation before Betty turned to Kath and asked, 'So, your husband, Dave, is it? Is he not able to be with you today?'

'Housebound, now. Been a diabetic all his life and hasn't really looked after himself properly, with eating and drinking and that, and now he's losing the use of his legs. Nerve damage, see and ulcers. On his legs. Like you wouldn't believe. Has the health visitor come twice a week to dress them.' Kath looked at Sarah.

'I'll just go and check where you've got to go.' And with that, Sarah was up and off again.

Kath looked at Betty. 'He's a bit of a worry, too, if I'm honest. Sarah has no patience with him. Thinks he brought it on himself. The health visitor, too. She never says anything but I'm sure she thinks it.'

'Yes, it must be difficult for you,' said Betty. 'How long have you been married?'

'Thirty-seven years. Thirty-eight in September.'

'That's a long time,' said Betty. 'You've stuck by him, then. Can't always have been easy.'

'Had to, really,' said Kath. Betty looked into her face for meaning and saw regret. Betty said nothing, allowing the silence to do its work.

'Can I tell you? Yes, I can. I feel I can tell you. Sarah doesn't know. None of them know.' Betty looked back, sage and trustworthy. 'I stole him off my best friend.'

'Oh,' said Betty.

'It was such a long time ago, now. I was very young. We'd never been allowed boyfriends – my dad never allowed it. I didn't get my first proper kiss till I was twenty. Then, when I was old enough to answer my dad back, I went a bit wild. Ran off with a boy from the fair, once! Making up for lost time, I was and I was always attracted to the bad lads – the ones with a bit of sparkle and dash. My friend Sally – she was my best friend, really, in those days – she started seeing this boy and I thought he was the bee's knees. Ever so good-looking and dressed a lot in leather – 'ad a motorbike, see. Anyway, she started seeing him and they were going out together, for a few weeks and then she told me they'd 'ad a row and she didn't want to see him again.'

'And you took her at her word?' said Betty. It wasn't really a question.

'Yes,' said Kath. 'I thought the field was clear. Looking back now, I see that I wanted it to be clear. I was so attracted to him. It caused an 'ell of a stink, first between me and Sally and then between all our other friends and I've not spoken to Sally from that day to this. When I fell pregnant with Josie – that's Sarah's and Simon's sister – we had to leave Colley and that's when we moved to Langwith. Into a council 'ouse and we've been there ever since.'

'But you've made a go of it since?' said Betty, 'and raised three kids and nursed each other through illnesses and coped with your mum and dad's rejection.'

'Yes, that's right,' said Kath, 'but how did you know about that?'

'It's not that hard to guess,' said Betty, 'given how your dad was about boyfriends.'

'No, I suppose not,' said Kath.

'And you've been happy, since?' asked Betty.

'Yes, yes, by and large,' said Kath. 'All marriages have their ups and downs and it's not always been easy, especially not when Dave was drinking, but we're through that now, and we rub along.'

'You used an interesting word earlier. You said you *stole* Dave from your friend Sally.'

'Yes, well I did,' said Kath.

'... almost as if Dave was an object.'

'Well, no, I didn't mean that,' said Kath.

'No, I'm sure you didn't,' said Betty, 'but I wondered if you'd ever considered that Dave is a human being, capable of making his own decisions, and he chose not to be with Sally and to be with you instead.'

'No, I 'adn't really thought of that,' said Kath. 'I've always been so wrapped up in thinking about Sally and how I wronged her.'

'... and did Sally ever get married?'

'Oh yes,' said Betty. 'In fact, she married one of my ex-boyfriends and they still live in Colley to this day. My mum used to keep me up to date on the goings-on. 'Ad three kids and now has grandchildren of her own, too.'

Betty said nothing and simply smiled at Kath.

'So you mean why don't I try getting back in touch with her and see if bygones can be bygones? You're right, yes of course I can do that!' And she smiled and looked about her and laughed out loud. 'Yes, yes, of course!'

'You've perked up,' said Sarah, returning once more to the table.

'Yes, thanks to Betty here.' And they both looked round.

Betty's chair was empty.

'Where'd she disappear to?' asked Kath, bewildered.

'Well, her name badge is still on the table,' said Sarah, picking it up. 'I'll take it through to the kitchen and give it back to her.' She got up again and walked over to the kitchen door with its 'Staff Only' notice firmly on the outside.

'Hello! Hello!' called Sarah, pushing the door ajar.

The door was pulled open from the inside and a man in chef's whites was standing there. 'Come in,' he said, 'what can we do for you?' Sarah momentarily wondered who the 'we' referred to, since she could see nobody else there.

'I've brought Betty's name badge back. Is she here?'

'Who?' asked the man

'Betty,' repeated Sarah. 'Is she here?'

'There's nobody of that name works here' said the man and stared at Sarah until she felt embarrassed.

'Betty. Her name's Betty. She tidies up the trays and keeps the café clean. She was just talking to my mother.'

The man just looked at her and Sarah could see that he was struggling to comprehend her words. There was a silence and then he said, 'Here let me see,' and held out his hand for the badge. Sarah turned it over to show him.

They both stared at it.

Beneath the crest and the words 'St Elizabeth's Hospital,' it was completely blank.

God in a Bandstand

Now, I don't know about you, but if I want to commune with God, I find a quiet place to go. In truth, I like churches but only when I've got them all to myself... and God, obviously. It's only then, when all the other braying noises of life can be temporarily switched off, that I can find the space God occupies and sit for a while with hem.

I use 'hem,' you'll have noticed – it's a bit pretentious, I know – but I do have a reason. That is because I think of God mostly as a masculine figure – long grey beard, Charlton Heston jawline and, for a reason I can't remember, dungarees. So the pronoun's got the start and finish of a masculine one but not a masculine centre. At the heart of God are a lot of female characteristics – anti-belligerence, empathy and, of course, love. Hence the middle of 'her' allied to the structure of 'him' equals 'hem.' You'll be pleased to know there'll be no other linguistic peculiarities to contend with. It's not Irvine Welsh.

The other background issue you'll need to be aware of is that I have a long-standing problem with evangelism. Evangelism, mind, not evangelists. They are simple souls who believe that we all need what they believe, in order to, for example, qualify for one of the 144,000 places available in Heaven. Or they're sixteen-year-old Elder Blinkelberry from Salt Lake City whose collar is still chaffing. Or they're frail old Jehovah's Witnesses round again for one last crack at bible jousting. No, I don't have any problem with them. They believe and I envy them their wholeness of hope. It's evangelism that's the issue – the very idea that you can infect someone else with faith.

So it is with some irritation, bordering on rancour that I observe the Christians who occupy the bandstand in the middle of the public park, in the middle of this small town, in the middle of Derbyshire, in the middle of England. They have planted themselves at the very centre of things to show off their Christian credentials and broadcast their piousness to anyone who's passing, drinking tea at the café or trying to hole a putt on a municipal-quality green. 'Look at us,' they silently cry, 'what worthy folk are we!'

I don't believe God actually occupies the bandstand or would ever think to visit. It's rather a draughty place, reasonably well maintained, it has to be said. Despite cutbacks, Derbyshire maintains its civic pride, usually by painting stuff. The bandstand's no exception – it's octagonal, black and white, and with a balustrade. No, the bandstand's not a forlorn desert. It's an elevated platform suitable for, amongst other things, bands to play on and for people to gather close by and watch, or even listen. But it is draughty. And that's why I think God wouldn't visit. You don't catch God in a breeze.

But, of course, I don't think the Bandstand Christians are bothered about that. They don't go there to meet God. They go to meet each other, amass themselves in a band of brothers and sisters and show off. Christianity, it would appear, has to be transacted in the plain sight of all, ascetically wind-whipped and three foot higher than anyone else.

'Well, OK,' you might say. 'Don't look. Avoid the park of a Sunday morning or walk round the perimeter. Why go out of your way to be offended? And, in any case, didn't you say it was evangelism and not the evangelists you had a problem with?'

Yes, well, in their case, it's much of a muchness. Evangelism writ large, as they call silently from their tower. Of a Sunday, I neither walk through the Park nor seek to see them from afar. I know that they are probably there, mid-Park, and am happy not to be.

I do, however, habitually, frequent a nearby café. It was, originally, at my wife's suggestion and we have rapidly become regulars, known by our first names and with predictable orders of cappuccino-and-two-slices-of-well-done-toast (her) and a-large-americano-and-a-bacon-cob (me). My wife never varies – she likes the consistency of things. I, however, have experimented with all sorts there – a full English (great even without beans), pains au raisin, eggs Benedict and sausage cobs

– but have learnt to come back to the bacon cobs. Three rashers of deliciously medium-fried bacon in a toasted ciabatta roll. Just a dab of brown sauce and they are rendered into a crescendo of flavours building heaven on my palate.. We take the papers and chat, or don't. Everything's easy, as it should be – it's Sunday.

So, dear reader, imagine my chagrin when, mid-roll, the Bandstand Christians walk in, make an awful lot of noise re-arranging tables into something altar-shaped and sit down to continue their theological pretences, not two yards away. In an instant, the words I'm juggling are dropped, the salty bacon I'm savouring is diluted and the gentle cocoon of Sunday morning is punctured. Of course, being Christians, too, their modus communicandi is far from sotto voce. No-one may be deaf to the Word of the Lord.

We're all preparing for death, each in our different ways, but they've already bought their tickets – and I don't mind that – but what I object to is the accompanying smugness. We, the rest of us, are probably going to the same concert, whoever's performing, but aren't sure where we'll be watching from. They're in the balcony with a perfect unobstructed view. They imagine that we'd also like to have that same view and that's where I part company. I'm happy to take my chances on a seat anywhere and want my pay-at-the-door spontaneity respected.

I'd also like my personal soundsphere respected; that is, I'd like them to speak at a volume which doesn't clamour for attention – my attention. I favour them with a cold look and, temporarily, make eye contact with the heartiest amongst them. I hold his gaze a fraction longer than is comfortable for either of us and hope that communication has been achieved. My wife sees this and tuts. She's no fan, either, but fights shy of conflict and disapproves of my obviously-demonstrated antagonism. I look at her and make a small Gallic gesture. Inside, of course, I'm a little startled by my own aggression and feel myself the lesser man. I return to my crossword and cob but the bacon now tastes salty.

1 Down: 'Decline evident in holy sisterhood' (5). My attention was drawn to this one; I'd already got 1 Across ('lachrymal') and having the first letter is always helpful, despite the fact that I've been doing cryptic crosswords for at least thirty-five years and am quite adept at the conventions. Perhaps, also, in the context of the row going on around me, the word 'holy' caught my eye. In any case, I focused my mind on it. The definition or meaning part is always at the beginning or at the end, so the answer would either mean 'decline' or 'sisterhood' or perhaps 'holy sisterhood.' I couldn't immediately think of any five-letter words beginning with 'l' that meant any of these things. I'd have to move onto analysis or skip to another clue.

Before I could do either, Mr Hearty was suddenly there looming above us. I looked up, slightly startled. 'Can I borrow your salt?' he beamed his most radiant smile.

'Yes,' I said. 'Here you are.' I reached out and lifted it up off the table for him. I looked into his eye, unsmiling.

'Oh, thank you so much,' he said and I looked for any sign that the emphasis was for sarcasm. I saw none. He was truly grateful for my small gift of salt. I despised him more.

'Anything else?' I offered with flat discourtesy.

'No, no, it was just salt we were missing. Thank you again.'

'Welcome,' I said. I watched him move off back to his table. 'Salt, anybody?' he boomed above the mounting cacophony. There were no takers. Apparently only he needed it – some people are never cured.

My wife looked across at me. I could see she was displeased and her flat mouth spoke volumes. There'd be no point in mounting a defence of my brusqueness and to do so would, in any case, imply that my behaviour had been less than perfect. Allied to which, they were sitting so close that our conversation would be overheard. I went back to 1 Down.

'Decline evident in holy sisterhood.' Still nothing was '*evident*' to me so I tried out the idea that 'in' might indicate that the answer was hidden inside another word or sequence of words. Beginning at the letter 'l,' I formed the word 'lysis (hidden in 'ho<u>ly-sis</u>terhood').' I hadn't heard of it but, if it were right, and that seemed possible, then it would have to mean 'decline.' In the modern world, dictionaries have been supplanted by mobiles but my own phone, dependent upon the whims of Three, would, I knew from past experience, find no connection in this café. My wife's phone, on the other hand, enjoyed the ubiquity of O2.

'Can you see if 'lysis' is a word?' I asked.

She favoured me with an uncomprehending look. 'What?'

'Lysis,' I said. 'L-Y-S-I-S' Is it a word?'

She reached down into her bag, in search of the phone.

'Oh yes!' boomed Mr Hearty, across the length of his table, the gap between tables, the width of our table and the heads of all those congregants and my bowing wife, 'Lysis is a word. It's from the Greek, meaning destruction.'

I looked across to find him sitting very upright and, once more, beaming like he was in an Alice in Wonderland audition. 'Lysis,' he repeated, 'destruction.' He was radiant with assuredness and something else – some small facial expression that spoke of the satisfaction he felt whenever his knowledge could be paraded. And, indeed, it was being paraded, judging by the numbers of adjacent customers who were now looking over in my direction.

I was completely flummoxed by this turn of events. I was quietly expecting my wife to come up with the answer which would be quietly transmitted across the table and the mystery of 1 Down would be resolved, … or it wouldn't. But, whatever, the outcome, it would be quiet. Now, it was as if the whole world (or, at least, this small corner of it) was being raucously advised of my ignorance versus his knowledge. My instinct was to loathing but my intellect was urging that social protocol be observed.

'Thank you,' I said, in a loud clear voice, looking fully at him.

He beamed all the more, maintaining eye contact until, finally, his gaze fell back upon those more closely around him.

'But I'll just check,' I announced, nodding in the direction of my wife's now-held phone.

He looked back up at me but now not so cocksure. He turned the beam back up but it was too late – we both knew I'd punctured him. I did not speak but maintained eye contact whilst smiling wanly. He kept up the beaming but, eventually, had to look down. There was a moment of silence amongst the congregants but then one of them, a youngish woman with bouncy hair and a polo neck, remarked that the coffee was particularly good and wondered if the café had changed the brand. No-one seemed to know but several agreed it was good coffee.

My wife had, by now, successfully inserted 'lysis' into Google and handed me the phone over to me without waiting for the results. Doubtless, she was feeling the pressure and wanted no part of the reveal. On the screen, I read the following: 'lysis n. Greek λύσις; *the disintegration of a cell by rupture of the cell wall or membrane*.'

I paused and, without looking up, made a sound which had two tones. I shrugged and sat back in my chair. Those congregants who were facing me stole glances, as did a couple sitting at a table some distance away. I let the moment hang, savouring the tension of the collective wonderment.

Mr Hearty glanced up and made eye contact. He was expecting great things.

'Thanks, anyway!' I called across.

Café Inglesh

Café Inglesh was situated at the end of a walkway leading down to the front at Mezcladañosa. A lot of pedestrian and moped traffic funnelled down there from the markets and main shopping areas in the high town, and, in consequence, the café was a thriving business and had been so, since it was first established, in Spring 1980, by Nicolau and Inês Picasso. Last summer, Nicolau and Inês had 'retired' and the running (though not the ownership) had passed on to their son Esteve and his wife Zuzen.

The café itself had two very distinct parts, each with its own clientele. Inside was dark and windowless with ochre-coloured paint on the rough-plastered walls and brown oak beams above and around. The walls bore testimony, everywhere, to the now-banned bullfighting with matadors in garish costumes posing, as bulls were duped. Pride of place amongst all this memorabilia was a picture of El Alfeñique ('The Weakling'), a bull of colossal proportions. The lighting was adequate to purpose, if that purpose was to see your companion's face and where your glass was. This was Nicolau's domain and had remained so through and beyond his 'retirement' and it was where he entertained his friends. He arrived, every day, shortly after the café opened, from the flat above, and took up his stool, at the corner of the bar, from where he could survey any and all passing matters. Zuzen placed a small black coffee in front of him and a Picardy glass of 'Bonet.'

The outside was a much brighter and gayer scene with multi-hued chairs and tables. It could be breezy, on occasions, but, in the height of the season, this was welcome. The umbrellas, uniformly advertising Estella Damm beer, kept the more extreme ravages of the Spanish sun at bay and made it habitable throughout the summer. This was the domain of the Brits, mostly expats, who had first come for the bacon and eggs but stayed for the butifarras. Every morning, promptly at 10.30ish, Esteve rolled up the new electric shutter and began the work of moving and organising tables and chairs as the café spilled outwards, just a metre or two beyond what had been agreed with the local council as the limit of their commercial area.

The name 'Café Inglesh' had been Nicolau's idea. He knew, instinctively, what his primary market was – the resident and itinerant British communities – but also wanted to placate his wife, a Portuguese whose fierce exterior belied a romantic core. He couldn't count how many 'sabelotodo[1]' Brits had, over the years, told him that 'Inglesh' was mis-spelt or advised him of how to translate the menu. He had smiled, thanked them all and changed nothing. He prided himself on knowing what his market was and how to service that. However, sometimes, there had been, on his part, a certain reluctance to make investments and satellite TV had been one such situation. He had wondered long and hard about how it might affect both the custom and atmosphere of the bar he had, over 15 years, built into a business serving both Brits and Catalans and didn't want to jeopardise that balance. However, Esteve had been a very vocal proponent, mustering all his 16 year-old's logic to persuade his father that it would be worth it for the Valencia games alone. Esteve had been allowed to win the day and, once Nicolau had adjusted to the noise levels, he could see how it boosted his income, particularly when Arsenal were playing.

***

Gordon knocked on the door of the flat he referred to as 'Casa Esmith' and, when Kath opened it, asked, 'Llest?' He pronounced it in the manner of Lurch answering the Addams Family doorbell.

'Preparat!' said Dawn. 'Esteve's told you a thousand and one times: local people say 'preparat,' not 'llest' and part of the reason for that is that 'llest' doesn't even mean 'ready,' it means smart, intelligent.'

---

1   know-all

'Tomaytoes, Tomates,' said Gordon. 'Anyway, where's Keith?'

'Dealing with last night's Chinese,' said Rosemary dismissively. 'He'll never learn. The doctor's told him but does he pay any attention? Does he heck!'

'Coming,' shouted a distant man's voice, echoing slightly. Rosemary and Dawn exchanged resigned looks. They had been married to Keith and Gordon long enough to enjoy disapproving of their husbands' more ridiculous behaviour. 'We'll walk on,' said Dawn, signalling to Rosemary, and the two women set off. Gordon was left in a social no-man's land and stepped out onto the landing in order to avoid having to witness any noises coming from the interior of the flat. 'Come on, mate!' he shouted. Keith took his time but appeared eventually. 'Better an empty house…' he said.

'… que un mal inquilini[2],' replied Gordon. Keith smiled.

On their way to the café, Keith and Gordon talked golf. It was the second day of the Spanish Open from Valderrama and there had been an unexpectedly poor showing from the big names of the European Tour, such that a little-known Englishman was leading the pack. Gordon and Keith agreed that he probably wouldn't be there, come Sunday, but, at least for now, it lent a bit of interest.

When they arrived at Café Inglesh, Rosemary and Dawn were already ensconced at their favourite table, near the bar but with the best view of the harbour, and chatting about a new couple who had just moved into

---

2   *than a bad tenant.*

the penthouse flat in a block adjacent to where they lived. Dawn was recycling gossip she'd heard, in the hairdresser's about the wife and Rosemary was trying out her theory about the origins of their wealth.

'Hola Gordón i Keet,' said Esteve.

'Hola, Esteve,' said Gordon, though Keith just nodded. He was reticent to compete with Gordon's Catalan and mildly irritated by being called 'Keet.'

'L'habitual?' enquired Esteve.

'Si, senyor!' said Gordon and looked to check with Keith. 'The usual?' he enquired.

'Yes, yes, even I know 'l'habitual,' said Keith. Gordon nodded to Esteve. 'L'habitual per a nos dos,' he said.

'And for the lovely ladies?' Esteve enquired, having walked, by now, over to their table. 'Just toast for me, please, Esteve,' said Dawn, 'two slices. What're you having, Rosemary?'

'A glass of orange juice, please,' said Rosemary, 'and bruschetta.'

'Ooo,' said Dawn, 'that sounds nice. Yes, I'll have that too. Bruschetta per a dos.' She smiled winningly at Esteve, who smiled back and turned to the bar.

'*Zuzen, bruschetta for the wrinklies and bacon-and-egg sandwiches for the potbellies, as per bloody usual*[3],' he said rapidly, conscious of Gordon's slowly growing knowledge of Catalan. He also ramped up the local accent, just for good measure. Zuzen nodded and went through to the kitchen.

---

3   Speech in *italics* represents a translation of what is said, between local people, in Catalan. It is rendered word for word.

'Bon dia, Senyor Picasso!' called Gordon to Nicolau, who nodded in the same stern-faced way that Zuzen had, but said nothing. He took a sip of his coffee and looked sagely out onto the scene.

'I can never tell with that guy,' said Gordon, sotto voce.

'No,' agreed Keith.

***

Nicolau had known Vicent and Ximo since schooldays. They'd been in the same football team, experimented with the same drugs and, on one occasion, ended up in the same prison cell, even if only for one night. Such experiences and the approximate equality in their lives and incomes had formed a strong bond between them.

'*So,*' said Ximo, drinking his second beer of the afternoon, '*confident?*'

'*Confident of what?*' asked Vicent.

'*Of winning Valencia?*'

'*No, not confident,*' said Vicent.

'*And you, Nico?*' Ximo asked looking at Nicolau. '*Usually you have a sense of those things.*'

Nicolau took a sip of his 'Bonet' and looked non-committal. '*Is difficult to say. According with the newspapers, the bats have lost many games narrow margin.*' He said the word 'bats' with sarcasm – 'bats' was newspaper language and the three of them had long ago agreed that the newspapers were all biased against Valencia.

'*But,*' said Ximo, '*the Whites have done well at the*

Cup. If Voro himself approaches to the game as a match of the Cup, they could win.'

'*Maybe,*' said Vicent, '*but the Yellow Submarine has won five of the last six matches. They are on the form.*'

Nicolau winced slightly and, he hoped, invisibly. He liked Vicent very much – indeed, he thought of Vicent, more than Ximo, as being like a brother – but he hated new expressions like 'Yellow Submarine.' Villarreal played in yellow so 'Groguets,' little yellows, was fine. '*Bah,*' he said with a shrug, '*we will see.*'

'*Is that at the television?*' asked Ximo.

'*Without doubt, is on the Sky,*' said Vicent.

'*Ourselves we will find here to watch it, no?*' asked Ximo, looking directly at Nico.

'*Is clear,*' affirmed Nicolau, '*we are to watch here, whatever that they those Brits want.*'

***

Sunday early afternoon found Gordon and Keith in the café, at a table a little way away from Nicolau, who was eating a plate of cod stew. Esteve had promised them that the golf would be on and, although he had needed reminding when they arrived, he had been quick to switch on the Sky box. Their predictions had been right and the first round leader had fallen by the wayside and the lead was now being contested by the regular money-earners. Gordon and Keith settled in for a long afternoon.

In the middle of the afternoon, they were joined by a small group of Irish golfers, who they'd met on the golf course the previous day and invited to come along. The Irish were lively and one of them in particular seemed very excited by the golf, shouting encouragement to Graeme McDowell and Rory McIlroy, as they drove and chipped, and holding his head and breath, as putts skimmed past the hole.

'Are you lads Ulstermen?' Gordon asked.

'Hell, no,' said the oldest of them (at least, judging by the hairline). 'We're all of us from Roscommon, although Aodhan here's moved away to the Big City,' he said.

'Dublin?' queried Keith.

'Ach no,' he said, 'Galway – I said the Big City, not the Metropolis.' He looked earnestly at Keith, who smiled wanly. Keith wasn't sure where Roscommon was and had only a vague notion of Galway. He tried to regain the initiative. 'No, I was just wondering why you're cheering on McDowell and McIlroy. They're both Northern Irish.'

'Well, you see,' Aodhan leaned in, 'we're all from the island of Ireland and, one day, we'll all be one Ireland together.' He fixed Keith with a stare that brooked no disagreement.

'I see,' said Keith.

By now, the bar area had started to fill up. Gordon and Keith recognised many of the locals. Several were tradespeople that Nicolau did business with and others were just friends and relatives. Inês appeared, too, which was very unusual in the afternoons, with another woman whom Gordon and Keith had never seen before.

'Bon dia, Senyora Picasso,' Gordon hailed her as she passed.

'Hello, Mr Jones' said Inês, smiling but only at the mouth. She looked at him for a moment and saw that he was looking at her companion. 'The weather is good today, isn't it? Not too hot nor too cold. How is it for you?'

'Yes, yes, it's lovely,' he agreed, bringing his gaze back to Inês.

'Well then, enjoy your afternoon, everyone,' she said and, with that, left their table, with the other woman in tow. Gordon watched her go.

'*The what he wanted?*' asked Nicolau, when the two women reached his stool.

'*He wanted to know who was Aurora but not himself dared to ask. The his tongue was hanging out.*'

'*Malparit[4]!*' was Nicolau's verdict. '*Esteve, go to tell to the losers that the match is on in five minutes.*'

Esteve sighed but walked over to the table. 'Do you wish more drinks, gentlemen?' They did and five more bottles of Estrella were ordered. '*Five Estrellas, Zuzi, please*' he called across the bar before turning back to the table. 'I'm afraid, gentlemen that will begin soon the match and the golf will close.'

'Really, Esteve?' Gordon put on his best theatrical tone. 'Why is that?'

'Because is the match with Villarreal,' explained Esteve, 'is, 'ow you say, derby.' He pronounced it in the American way.

'Oh, you mean it's a derby,' said Keith, all but imitating Brian Clough in his pomp.

---

4   Bastard

'Yes, si, a derby. Villarreal is close, is 60km but really is a fight between Germans.'

'Germans?' queried Gordon, 'why would Germans be involved?'

'Yes, Germans – men with the same father. 'Hermanos' in Espanish.'

'Ah, brothers,' said Gordon.

'Yes, si, brothers. The brothers Roig. Francisco at Valencia and Fernando at Villarreal. They fight. Valencia still is the big club and Villarreal is the little but are nearly equal now and so they fight.'

'I see,' said Gordon, reflecting that he may just have caught something of the story on the local news but, more than anything, feeling blindsided by his own ignorance. He liked to have the last word in conversations and now he wasn't going to.

Esteve smiled and walked away.

***

Gordon, Keith and the now temporarily silent Irishmen, turned their full attention to the screen, as if to drink in as much information as they could before the well was capped. Unfortunately, there was no immediate shot of the leaderboard but there was a Spanish commentator and Gordon was able to piece together just enough to tell his tablemates that the first six players were separated by three strokes and they included Andrew Johnston and Sergio Garcia but that McIlroy and McDowell were not mentioned.

At that moment, the channel switched and the screen

was filled with the raucous passion of the Mestalla faithful. Keith glanced across at Nicolau whose attention was firmly on the television, but was also, it seemed to Keith, smiling slightly. Just as Keith was turning back to the table, he thought he saw Nicolau look across from the corner of his eye, but, when he turned back to check, Nicolau's gaze was, once again, front and centre. You couldn't tell with that guy.

'Anyway,' said Gordon to all assembled, 'what shall we do? Stay and sit out the football till the golf comes back on or go see if we can find another bar?'

'Well,' said one of the Irishmen, 'I'm going nowhere till this drink's finished.' His compatriots agreed and so Gordon and Keith resigned themselves to staying put.

Gordon took the opportunity to look around and noticed that all the tables were now full of men and many more were standing on the boundary between inside and outside. Apart from one table of Dutch cyclists nearby, there was now a solid sea of Catalans gathered to witness the game.

At the table nearest to him, Gordon recognised two brothers who he had seen carrying out plumbing work for Esteve. He had seen them at the Café over a period of several weeks and felt almost as if he knew them. As he looked across, one of the brothers turned and nodded to him.

'Bon dia,' ventured Gordon.

'Bon dia,' came the reply and the man's brother also looked over. Gordon nodded to him, as well, and the nod was returned.

'Partidaris València[5]?' queried Gordon. He pronounced the 'd' in the usual English way, instead of as 'th,' as the locals do.

'Yeth,' said the man, 'we are.'

'Bo,' said Gordon and turned back to his table, oblivious to the sarcasm.

'Who's that?' whispered Keith.

'They're plumbers. Do a lot of work here. Haven't you seen them around?'

'Not really,' said Keith and tuned back into the television in order to see if there was, in fact, anything remotely enjoyable or entertaining about football. The game itself had just kicked off and Keith looked for pattern and action in what he could see but found his attention drawn more to the crowd scenes, with their enormous flags and orchestrated chants. Maybe, he thought, it'd be good to go along, sometime, just for the spectacle.

'*For what are you talking with the gay?*' asked his brother.

'*He not is gay,*' said the first man. '*Not all the people are homosexual English.*'

'*He watches of golf,*' said the brother, '*and now that he will leave for the fact that the football is on. Gay.*'

'*You are ridiculous of sometimes.*' He looked at his brother pityingly but his brother just shrugged and turned back to the football. A few moments passed but the football did not sparkle.

'*As more it has better, the Brits leave the EU,*' said the

---

5   Valencia supporters?

brother. '*Never themselves join in with other countries. They are arrogant. Like gays.*'

The first man stared at his brother and mused that it was very surprising how two people who had grown up in the same family could have such different views. He loved his brother but, on occasions, he didn't much like him. He turned his attention back to Gordon. 'Senyor!' he called across to Gordon, who turned and placed his palm on his chest to check that the man was, indeed, talking to him.

'Yes, si,' said Gordon.

'¿Dóna suport vostè Brexit[6]?' he asked.

'No, jo no support Brexit,[7]' Gordon paused for maximum effect, 'però, llavors, no sóc gai[8].'

This drew one or two inquisitive stares from Catalans at adjacent tables but the plumber's brother kept his own eyes firmly on the TV screen. The plumber nodded and smiled weakly. Gordon turned back to the table.

'What was that about?' asked Keith.

'Just a little confusion over who might vote for Brexit,' said Gordon, 'but it's resolved now.' Keith could see, from Gordon's face, that there was no mileage in pursuing it further and drank his beer, instead. He watched the match and could start to sense, more from the crowd in the café than the game itself, that something was starting to build. He did notice that the team in yellow seemed to be all grouped together and the team in white were passing the ball around between themselves. He was still

---

6   Do you support Brexit?

7   No I don't support Brexit.

8   but, then, I'm not gay.

unsure how to interpret this, though. His pondering was interrupted by the appearance at his shoulder of one of the Dutch cyclists.

'I'm shorry to interrupt,' said the lycraed figure, 'but do you guys know of anywhere where we could buy some gear?'

There was no immediate reply, as Keith, Gordon and the Irishmen all processed his request and wondered what exactly he was referring to. Gordon thought he'd play it safe. 'There's a garage, up in the town, straight up the hill (he pointed), which does a sideline in cycle repairs and cycle gear,' he said. 'They might help you but you'll have to hurry – they'll be closing soon.'

'Shorry, you mishunderstand me,' said the man. 'I didn't mean shycling,' and, with that, he made a gesture of smoking a cigarette whilst inhaling deeply and raising his eyebrows.

'Aaah,' said Gordon, 'I'm sorry, I don't…'

Before he could finish his sentence, Aodhan interjected: 'Sure, I have some myself. Shall we?' and nodded in the direction of outdoors. 'Shure,' said the cyclist and they both got up and walked outside. Keith and Gordon exchanged glances but, since neither of the other Irish lads appeared bothered, thought it best to keep their own counsel.

***

The match progressed with, mostly, Valencia pressing and with each attack, the noise level in the bar rose but fell back again when the attack came to nothing. Keith was starting to understand, from the reactions of those around him, how pressure could build and that there was tension, even if there weren't any goals. He was just starting to see how football might be appealing, when the team in yellow broke forward quickly and one of them, the one with the No. 9 on his shirt, scored. Distant cheering was heard on the TV but, in Café Inglesh, there was only silence before a torrent of what Keith took to be invective.

'What are they saying?' he asked Gordon.

'Lots of bad words, Keith, lots of bad words,' said Gordon authoritatively, although, in truth, he recognised only 'fill de puta[9].'

The team in white kicked off again, hardly noticed by the café's patrons but, before two passes had been played, the referee blew loudly three times and the teams trailed off for half-time.

'Well,' said one of the Irishmen, 'more drinks?' and, before waiting for an answer, signalled over to the bar. He held up a bottle of Estrella in one hand and five outstretched fingers on the other. Zuzen nodded, uncapped five bottles and placed them on a tray, where they stayed for several minutes before Esteve finished his conversation with a group of his friends and came to deliver them.

'Could I bother you to bring us over some glasses for the beer?' asked one of the Irishmen politely of Esteve.

9   'Son of a bitch' is the literal translation, but its strength is greater than those words imply in English.

Esteve was, at first, puzzled by the request but understood the word 'glasses' and went over to the bar to fetch them.

'Now, then,' said one of the Irishmen, 'how's about we get into some proper lushing?' and, with that, he produced a half bottle of Bushmills from his jacket pocket. He raised his eyebrows and beamed at Gordon and Keith. They shrugged, since the bottle was already poised at the lip of Gordon's glass and accepted their fate. Generous servings of Bushmills were topped with lager and consumed full-throatedly by all. 'That's the spirit!' said the Irishman.

Gordon and Keith felt the immediate surge of alcohol in their veins and smiled broadly at each other and their benefactors. 'Let's see if the Dutch lads want to join us,' suggested Gordon and was up and out of his seat before waiting for any acknowledgement, much less agreement. The Dutch cyclists were, at first, reticent, but were encouraged by the gesturing of Aodhan and the others and, after a few seconds, came over. Accommodating them at the same table caused a little commotion and Nicolau cast an eye over in their direction, but the manoeuvre was accomplished without too many ruffled Catalan feathers.

'So, are you boys football fans, too?' asked Keith.

'Yesh, we're from Tilburg in the shouth of Holland, so we shupport Willem Twee,' said one of the other cyclists. Seeing the blank faces, he went on: 'It's the local team from Tilburg. Willem Twee means William the Second, the father of William the Third who became your king.

'No, not ours. Maybe theirs,' said one of the Irishmen

who hadn't, till that point, had very much to say for himself. He gestured in the direction of Gordon and Keith.

'No, yoursh as well,' said the Dutchman. 'In the seventeeth century, Ireland was still part of Britain.' The Irishman looked evenly at the Dutchman but said nothing. 'Yes, you're right,' said Keith, 'we didn't go our separate ways till about a hundred years ago.' Then, quickly, to fill the ensuing silence, added, 'But we've remained friends since.'

'Here's to the Irish!' said Gordon, holding his glass aloft.

'To the Irish!' said the Dutchman and everyone joined in, even the Irish. 'Another drink?' said Aodhan, looking round excitedly and, without waiting for confirmation, turned to the bar and shouted across to Zuzen 'Nou cerveses, si us plau[10].' Zuzen gestured to Esteve to come over to the table, perhaps because she wasn't sure she'd heard correctly or, more likely, because she wasn't used to being hailed across a crowded bar.

**

The second half rolled forward with Valencia gradually establishing control of the game and, with ten minutes to go, they scored. The bar erupted into a mini Mestalla of noise, hugging, beer-spilling and dad-dancing as the locals greeted the goal like a prodigal returning. Gordon and Keith, who, by this time, had consumed twice as

10   Nine beers, please.

much beer and many times more whisky than was their norm, were on their feet, too, completely embroiled in Catalan joy. The chant of 'Somos Nosotros'[11] broke out and swelled and Gordon and the rest of the table joined in. Keith looked at his friend and Gordon exaggerated the pronunciation for his benefit. Far quicker than he would ever normally join in with any collective group activity, Keith found himself singing along, buoyed by alcohol, the simplicity of the words and the 'Quanta La Mera' tune so beloved of football fans everywhere.

It took quite a while for the chanting to subside and, by the time everyone had resumed their seats and perches, the game had already kicked off again. There was a strange hush as, once more, Valencia pressed and the Villarreal players defended ever more desperately. The TV coverage cut frequently to the crowd, as 50,000+ people sought by scarf-waving, willpower and voice to push the ball into the Villarreal goal. The noise in the bar started to grow again and there was collective head-holding as a shot whistled over the bar.

'This is fantastic!' said Keith to Gordon. 'I've never been anywhere like this in my whole life!'

'No, it's fantastic!' agreed Gordon.

Another hush fell as, almost inexplicably to any of the patrons, Villarreal suddenly counter-attacked and, but for a late saving tackle by a Valencia defender, would almost certainly have scored. The ball broke to the Valencia keeper who threw it rapidly out to the wing. The hubbub in the bar grew again as the full-back sprang

11   We are (Valencia)

forward and, leaping two lunging tackles, sped to the byline. He crossed the ball diagonally back to where a Valencia player, on the edge of the area, launched himself at the ball. Forehead hit ball. Ball hit net.

The bar exploded with joy. Everyone was on their feet. The Irishmen were dancing a jig. Gordon and Keith were hugging Catalan men they wouldn't normally dare to do more than nod at. Even the sanguine Dutchmen were stood waving their arms in the air and joining in enthusiastically with 'Somos Nosotros.' Across, by the bar, Nicolau, Ximo and Vicent were alternating between dancing some form of jig and hugging one another. Keith found Gordon and directed his gaze over towards the bar. They stood and watched, for a moment, as Nicolau danced round behind the bar and took his wife's hand, led her out into the bar and danced with her some more.

Seeing his chance, Gordon made his way over to where Aurora was standing alone behind the bar.

'Senyora?' said Gordon, but then communicated the rest of his invitation by gesture, smile and eye gaze alone. Aurora looked back at him blankly, for a moment, before a smile melted across her face.

***

The next morning found Gordon way too early. His head had turned to stone and he was ready for death. Dawn offered him only the solace that could be found in a glass of water and two paracetamol and, once they had been taken, he felt in need of some strong black coffee.

'I think I'll see if Keith fancies a coffee,' he told Dawn, who smiled at him thinly.

On their way to the café, Keith was equally leaden of foot and mind and their conversations were intermittent as each searched for memories of the evening. From the moment the Bushmills was introduced, there was an ever denser haziness about exactly what had transpired and neither had any recollection whatsoever of how they had got home. Keith thought he remembered dancing with Nicolau in some weird variant of a samba and Gordon thought he might have kissed a woman but her face was vague and unrecognised. Neither, of course, spoke of these things, restricting themselves to banalities about how great an evening it had been.

On arrival, they sat just inside the front of the café, both feeling the need to be out of the sun but both, also, wanting to know whether their new positioning might be welcomed.

'Good morning, gentlemens,' greeted Esteve, 'and how are you?'

'Yes, we're fine, Esteve, thank you,' said Gordon. 'Please could we have two large coffees.' He indicated with his fingers the size of cup. 'Gran. Gran,' he emphasised.

Whilst Esteve was fetching the coffees, Gordon and Keith both sat looking outwards, neither speaking. Each was in a world of his own but each, too, was in the same world of pain and nausea: in a spreading, pulsing pandemic of discomfort. Just at the moment when both felt themselves furthest from whatever rescue strong black Catalan coffee might bring, the door from the upstairs flat opened and Nicolau and Inês stepped out. Inês took his arm and they walked, heads high, across and into the café. As they entered, Nicolau glanced across and stared, for a second, flatly, at them. He nodded but did not smile. Inês did not even nod.

'Looks like things are back to frosty,' said Keith.

'Yes,' said Gordon.

Esteve arrived with the coffees and the two cupped their drinks gratefully. The hot liquid stung their lips and the bitter coffee parched their tongues but somehow, above all else, the warmth of the cups brought succour. Survival assured, Gordon and Keith were able, finally, to look at each other and smile.

'What a night!' said Keith.

'Yes,' said Gordon.

And it was at that moment, that they noticed Nicolau looking directly across the room at them. They returned his gaze and each propelled a smile to their faces. Nicolau picked up his glass of 'Bonet' and raised it in tribute to them. They each made a gesture with open palms to indicate that they could not return the gesture, having no alcohol to hand. Nicolau shrugged but smiled too.

'You can never tell with that guy,' said Keith.

'No,' said Gordon.

Town View Café

She approached the table. 'What can I get you, gents?'

'Two breakfasts, please… with tea.' said Andy. He'd already heard me say what I wanted.

'Half-and-half or…?' she enquired.

'No. No, just beans.'

She turned her head to me. 'Yeah, me too, just beans.'

'OK,' and she was off, back to the kitchen. She disappeared just as she had appeared.

'Half-and-half?' I said.

'Beans and tomatoes' said Andy. 'I don't really approve.' Andy often said such things when he meant that he didn't like something. Perhaps he found it easier to express a morality than a preference.

'No,' I said.

The teas came first. The toast came next. Trailers to tempt us into the main feature. Breakfasts did arrive but they were for two women sat at a nearby table. The anticipation built…

To distract myself as much as Andy, I took to gossip. 'She's not keen on that woman.' I nodded in the general direction of the door and kept my voice low.

'How do you know?' Andy asked.

'She… the woman… just asked for two or three things in a row and she… the woman serving… said 'Yes, OK' to her but, when she turned away, she did this.' I raised my eyebrows, flattened my mouth, and looked upwards and to the left. Andy smirked. He observed the woman via the mirror on the back wall but said nothing.

Other conversation sparked up and broke down. A man took his son to the toilet. Another man arrived with a box of something for which he was thanked but not paid. A girl wandered around on her phone and looked this way and that but did not focus. The bonhomie expressed down the phone seemed like a performance. I wondered if the girl on the other end thought so too.

The breakfasts finally arrived in relay – Andy's first, then mine. 'Mind the plates – they're very hot!' she warned. We agreed to do so.

'Ooo,' I said, 'fried bread, too. I love fried bread.'

'Yes,' said Andy, 'always a bonus.' No need for morality now.

It was at the precise moment of starting to eat that I became aware of someone else having walked into the café. I glanced up and thought he resembled someone I knew but paid him no particular heed. The beans and fried bread were too good a combination to waste time on strangers. Andy, too, looked in the mirror at the newcomer but, unlike me, he stopped eating and put his fork back down.

'Now, then, my lovely!' boomed a voice.

I looked up then, my memory sparked by the vowels and intonations made familiar by hundreds of video clips. 'Bloody hell!' I whispered to Andy, 'it's…'

'Tommy Woodward!' the waitress exclaimed. 'Dad! Dad! Come quick! That fella from up the road's just come in!'

An older man (her dad, for sure) came out from the kitchen, round the counter, and stepped lively towards the man. 'Tommy!' he said, almost shouting. 'How the hell are you, boy?'

'Fine, fine, thanks, Jack,' came the reply. 'How are you? You're looking well.'

'Oh, not so bad. Can't grumble,' said Jack. 'How's your sister? I heard about her husband. Terrible business.'

'It's Tom Jones,' said Andy to me quietly. 'He's from Treforest… originally. Comes back from time to time. His sister still lives here.'

I looked over at him. Smaller than he looks on telly, I thought. Still the big chest though and that gaze – full-faced and unafraid. Grey but magnificent, an alpha male amongst alpha males, even though, in the present company, there wasn't much challenge. He looked over and I smiled, despite myself. I don't hero-worship and I was slightly disgusted at my own nascent sycophancy. He looked back at Jack.

'Yes,' he said but no more. There was a pause. 'Still here, then? Still churning out the breakfasts and fish and chips and all the other stuff,' he said, sweeping his arm broadly at the array of foodstuffs on display.

'Yes, yes. I'll be here till I die,' said Jack, resignedly. Jack looked down and I sensed regret and shame in his manner.

'Come on, now!' admonished his daughter, 'let's have no talk of that. Tom's back and we want to hear all about it. So, Tom, what's the reason for the visit? Family, is it?'

'Well, yes, of course, I'll be popping in to see them, if I have time, but they're doing a programme on me, CBS like, and they want to film me, back where it all began.'

'Another one!?' How many's that?' asked Jack, incredulous. 'It can't be five minutes since you were here doing the same thing for some other American station.'

'Well, when you get to my time of life, Jack, you can't afford to turn anything down. Who knows how long the voice's going to last?'

'It's still going, Tom,' said the daughter.

'What is?'

'*The Voice*. It's still on. But they got Boy George in to replace you,' she said. 'Bit of a difference.'

Tom looked at her, bemused. Of course, he knew all of that or, if it had temporarily slipped his mind, he at least knew that he was no longer on it. I could see, though, that he was unsure how the conversation had reached this point, much less how he was going to get out of it.

Fortunately for him, I thought, the daughter helped him out. 'So, are you taking them to the chapel, then?'

'Oh, yes, there and one or two of the working men's clubs,' said Tom. 'Looking forward to it.'

'You'll be lucky,' said Jack, 'with the working men's clubs. Most of them have shut down, now, see. Couldn't keep going, with all the cutbacks. No money in people's pockets, see, so they can't afford to go out, so much, these days.'

'No,' said Tom but you could tell he no longer had any real sense of what it might be like not to go out whenever you fancied it. He looked a bit wistful, I fancied, at that moment. Back, he was, here re-connecting but not immediately liking what he was re-connecting with.

Just then, a middle-aged man burst in through the door, looked at Tom, turned round and immediately shot out again. As the door closed, you could hear him almost shouting into the phone 'Yes, yes, it is him! Come down quick!'

'They'll all be here, now,' said Jack. 'Now that word's got out.'

'Oh, I doubt it,' said Tom. 'No-one's much interested in me anymore. Last single only sold 50,000. I'm not flavour of the month, now, see.' There was altogether more Welshness in the accent and more sparkle in his eyes as he looked from Jack to his daughter and back again. He made no move to leave. 'Cup of tea going, is there?' he asked.

'You sit yourself down there,' said the daughter, pointing to the window seat, 'and I'll bring you one right over.'

92

Tom moved over to sit down. He took the side facing into the café, with his back to the window, initially, but then turned his body half-round so that he could, equally, look out into the street. He alternated his gaze between the inside and out, nodding at his fellow customers but, also, looking at the pedestrians coming up from town or out of the Park. Jack, meanwhile, stood motionless, in front of the counter, obviously unsure whether he should go and keep Tom company. Tom appeared not to notice.

'Just tea, is it, Tom?' asked Jack, eventually. 'Not fancy a bacon butty or a fry-up?'

'No, nooo,' said Tom, slightly disdainfully. 'Not long had my breakfast, ta.' He looked over at the remains of the breakfasts the two women had had and then up at the women. He didn't say anything but smiled wanly at them. They smiled back and the one facing him moved in her seat. Tom looked instantly away and out of the window once more.

There was tension now in the air, vying for prominence against the pervasive smell of frying. Tom sat, enthroned in the window seat. The other customers – me and Andy, the two women, the man with his little boy – all sat self-consciously silent or making staccato conversation.

'Who's that man, Daddy?' the little boy's voice shrilled above the hubbub and cut immediately through the tension. All around, now, were smiles, as people relaxed, rescued by a child's naivety.

'He's just a singer, from round here,' deadpanned his

dad, unsmiling. Me and Andy exchanged a smirk and the two women spluttered. Tom looked over at the man and boy and smiled flatly. He turned away to look out of the window and, after a few seconds, turned back to face them again.

'Not a fan, then?' said Tom, 'Don't blame you – I sometimes wonder why I still do it.' The self-deprecation of the words wasn't matched by the facial expression, as the eyes darted from one table to the next. The man said nothing.

'Oh, come on,' said one of the women, 'Tom, can I call you 'Tom,' Tom, your last album was fabulous, lush it was, all those wonderful gospel tunes.'

I made a face at Andy and shrugged my shoulders slightly. Andy said, sotto voce, that a recent album had been full of traditional songs, but that he didn't think it was gospel. More like redemption songs and re-workings of classics and traditional songs. He also thought it was a few years ago, so it might not have been his last album.

'Thank you,' said Tom to the woman. 'I'm glad you liked it. It certainly brought back memories – recording it did – of playing and singing round here… and here I am, again, back home.'

'Oh yes,' said the woman, suddenly emboldened, 'I particularly liked that last track – 'Running,' was it? Wonderful tune. Is that your favourite?'

'Actually, it was called 'Run On,' if you're thinking of the last track, but I loved all of them and we got all the tracks down in two days, so it was real easy.'

'Aaah,' said the woman, clearly unfamiliar with the processes of recording music, 'well, anyway, that was my favourite… and my mum's.'

Tom looked wistful and gave a slight shake of the head. 'Oh good,' he said. 'I'm glad she liked it.' He wasn't. Not that he was unhappy that this unknown woman's unknown mother liked his music – well, that track in particular – but that he was finding it hard to imagine who this mother might be, much less her musical preferences. He stared momentarily at the woman and narrowed his eyes slightly. Perhaps he was working out whether he could or should say more. Perhaps he was wondering whether she was taking the piss, connecting his musical genre to an older generation. Perhaps he was recognising one of the perennial difficulties of dealing with the verbally agile folk of South Wales – the potential they have to blindside you, at any given moment, with an observation of hollowing honesty.

'Here's your tea, Tom,' said the waitress, 'and I put you some toast up, too, just in case, like.' She placed the tea and a plate of white toast on the table.

'Oh, smashing. Thanks,' said Tom, a little unsure whether he could stomach the cotton wool texture of British bread. He made no initial move towards either and looked up at the waitress and smiled. She turned away and went back into the kitchen. He picked up the cup and blew over its surface gently before taking a sip. He eyed the toast.

Just then, the door opened rather forcefully and a gaggle of four teenage girls spilled into the café, pushing and remonstrating loudly. Having announced their arrival, they were suddenly silent. One of them wandered over to where we were sitting and looked at us, in that way short-sighted people have. Realising that we weren't the object of her fascination, she turned back and rejoined her friends all, now, standing by the counter.

'What can I get you, girls?' asked the waitress.

'Two cans of coke and four straws, please,' said the girl who had reconnoitred us.

'Is that it?' said the waitress, trying (perhaps for Tom's sake) but failing to keep exasperation from her tone.

'Yes, that's it, ta,' said the girl.

'£2.20,' said the waitress, holding out her hand.

'What!' exclaimed the girl. '£2.20! That's extortionate.'

'Well,' said the waitress, 'that's the price here. If you want to go to McColl's, I'm sure it's cheaper there but this is a café, not a shop.'

The unblinking look said 'don't mess with me' but the girl looked like she wasn't used to being intimidated by adults. She paused for a moment, weighing up her options.

'Oh, stop messin', Nat,' said one of her mates. 'Here, I'll pay,' and she reached over and placed some coins into the waitress' still outstretched hand.

'Ta,' said the waitress, without breaking her gaze. Nat scoffed and turned away. The waitress raised an eyebrow and put the money in the till.

The girls made for an empty table, two away from where Tom was sitting, and sat down, hutching along the leatherette benches. They opened the cans noisily and shared their drinks with each other, leaning over the table.

'Those girls are naughty.' It was the little boy again.

The girls all turned to look at the little boy and his father. One of them stuck her tongue out at the boy.

'Look!' said the boy. 'Dad, did you see what she just did? Stuck her tongue out, she did! That's very rude, isn't it, Dad? Tell her, Dad.'

'Come on,' said the man, standing up. 'Let's go. It's time we were at your nan's.' He glared at the little boy so that he knew protest was futile. They stood up, paid and left but not before the little boy had given the girls the finger.

'You little bastard!' shouted Nat after the retreating boy but too late, seemingly, for his father to hear.

'Come on, girls, please,' said Tom. 'No need for language like that, here.' He favoured them with a smile and an imploring look.

Nat stared across. 'Are you that singer, then?' she challenged.

'Yes I am,' he said flatly, 'that singer.' He rolled the last words around his mouth.

'What's your name, then? Are you on telly or something? Are you from round here?' Nat hit him with a barrage of inquiry.

'I'm from Treforest, originally, so, yes, I'm from round here and, yes, I've been on the telly.'

'And what's your name?' Nat hadn't forgotten her first question.

'Tom. Tom Jones. Well, Tommy Woodward, as was.'

'So why did you change your name? What's wrong with 'Tommy Woodward'?'

'It was my manager's idea. He thought it'd make me sound more heroic,' Tom explained.

'Well, it doesn't. Makes you sound boring, really. Tom Jones. Very ordinary.'

'Well, he's far from ordinary,' Jack interjected. He'd been stood at the kitchen doorway but now came out into the café proper. 'He's done extraordinary things. Been to America. Lives there. Met Elvis. He was in the charts – 'Delilah,' 'It's Not Unusual,' 'Green Green Grass of Home.' Ever heard of them?' Jack enquired of Nat.

'No, I haven't but I think my nan has,' Nat smirked.

The other girls burst into laughter. Nat smiled, glorying in her smartness.

'Anyway,' she continued, 'bet you don't live in this dump any more, do you? Bet you've moved into some swanky place. I bet you live in London, don't you?' Nat was insistent.

'No, no, I don't live in London. Don't really like the place. Like Jack said, I live in LA.'

Nat and the girls were temporarily silent.

'My dad lives in LA,' offered one of the other girls. The others looked at her blankly. 'Yeah, he does,' she went on, 'Los Angeles – it's on the West Coast. It's where Hollywood is and Malibu and it was where 90210 was shot.' No-one said anything. This was clearly more information than any of them had realised she knew.

'Yeah, right, Rhi,' said Nat.

'Yeah, right,' said the girl – Rhi, apparently. There was a pause. 'Am I wrong?' Rhi turned to Tom. 'You live there. Am I wrong?'

'No, no,' said Tom, 'that's right. That's all right.'

'See,' said Rhi.

The door opened again and a couple walked in, followed in quick succession by another couple and a third. Over the course of the next five minutes, a stream of people walked into the café and, soon, all the tables were occupied. It was as if a social vacuum had suddenly become manifest in the town and people were drawn in to fill it. But that wasn't quite the image that came to my mind. It reminded me of the stream of bullfrog tadpoles you get when the male bullfrog realises that the pool all his offspring are in is going to dry up unless he opens up a channel to a larger pool. All these folk with their half-formed lives were responding to the daddy bullfrog sitting on his window throne.

Jack came out from the kitchen and smiled to himself – he'd predicted this. The waitress busied herself taking orders and the girls quietened down and drank their cokes without very much more audible to say. It did seem, though, that the three other girls were quizzing Rhi about her father and her new-found exoticness, even if only by association.

Tom turned, once more, to look out of the window.

'Blimey!' said Andy. I jumped slightly and realised that my attention had been so focused on all these other conversations that Andy and I had not been talking.

'What?' I said, rather tersely.

'Well,' he said, 'it's not every day I'm in the presence of a popstar... even if it's only hometown boy Tom Jones, grazing once more on the green, green grass.'

'It's not *only* Tom Jones,' I said. 'He was big in the sixties. I never liked his stuff – torturous ballads and the like – but he played big concerts and probably sold enough records back then to retire... Then he made a comeback, didn't he, in the nineties – that song with The Cardigans and he released a CD of duets with various people... I'd say he was a big star.'

'Yes,' said Andy, 'but he's gone off the boil now.'

'He's seventy-odd!' I said. 'I might have gone off the boil, myself, by then.' Andy raised an eyebrow but said nothing more.

'To-om,' implored one of the newly-arrived contingent, standing and walking over to his table, 'would you sign this for me? Please.' She held out in front of her a CD and stared adoringly at Tom.

'Yes, of course, my lovely,' said Tom, 'do you have a pen?' The woman looked alarmed and turned back to her table.

'Quick!' she said to the man sitting there, 'Pass me my bag.' He did and she made an elaborate search of its contents. Her hand emerged with nothing and she froze momentarily before a smile lit up her face. She put her hand back into the bag and pulled out a lipstick.

'This'll do, won't it?' she thrust the lipstick at Tom.

'Well, sure,' said Tom and began to write on the CD case.

'No, no!' said the woman, her mask of politeness slipping. 'Will you take out the sleeve notes and sign those? Please. The writing'll rub off if it's just on the outside, see?'

Tom eyed her and there was a scintilla of frustration but Tom was, inured by more than fifty years of responding to fans, no doubt aware of the constant need to placate them. Sales depended on them, after all and, as he said himself, who knew how long the voice would last…?

He opened out the sleeve notes and, in lurid pink, scrawled some long-practised approximation of his signature across them. He went to fold the notes back up but the woman reached out and took them from him before he could do so. 'That's fine,' she said. 'I'll just let it dry before I fold it up. Thank you.' She turned away and went back to her seat, raising her eyebrows to the upper limit of their range, as she did so. The man at her table looked sheepish as she sat back down. She waved the sleeve notes ostentatiously around and grinned at him. He looked back flatly, unsmiling, embarrassed, jealous.

The woman's enquiry had, clearly, now legitimised any form of contact because, barrelling across the entire café now came a sonorous voice, full of the flinty intonation of Valleys folk. 'Give us a song, Tom!' It was less a request than a command.

Tom smiled broadly. These were his folk, his clan, his heritage, asking him to do what he did best, to show off just like he had for his mother, in her kitchen, all those years ago. I thought he'd brush it away, feigning tiredness, modesty, or the need to preserve his voice for some upcoming recording session. But no…

'Waddudya like to hear?'

'Whatever you'd like, Tom.' The tone of the man's voice betrayed his delight, initially, but the final 'Tom' was deadpanned.

'Well, ' announced Tom, 'how about this old classic?' and launched off into the song I have known, since childhood, as 'Bread of Heaven' but which I know, through watching the rugby and the Treorchy Male Voice Choir as 'Cwm Rhondda' – 'Rhondda Valley.' However, instead of 'Guide me, O thou Great Redeemer,' Tom was knocking out: 'Wele'n sefyll rhwng y myrtwydd. Wrthddrych teilwng o fy mryd…'

'Whoa, whoa, Tom, TOM! Let me stop you there,' came the voice of the man who had asked Tom to sing anything. It was surprisingly loud – loud enough to drown out Tom's resonant baritone and shut him up. Tom looked over, those fearless eyes burning bright once more.

'That's no good to us, Tom,' explained the man. 'Let's hear it in English, so we can really enjoy it.'

Tom cleared his throat, in that way much parodied by Rob Brydon. He looked around at the folk sitting at the other tables but they simply returned his gaze and looked expectant. The woman who'd asked for the autograph, smiled encouragingly and Nat, Rhi and the other girls stared blankly. Even Jack, behind his counter, was simply waiting.

Tom cleared his throat once more, stood, walked to the centre of the café and faced his audience. His eyes scanned the assembly, meeting their excited eyes with his resilient unabashed gaze. He breathed in deeply.

'Guide me, O Thou Great Jehovah, Pilgrim through this barren land...'

Après Tout

'Have you seen this? It might be fun,' Jane suggested, holding up a leaflet.

'What is it?' asked Mark, without reaching for it.

'It's advertising a quiz. There's going to be a quiz, a week on Tuesday. £10 a head but you get access to a running buffet and there's a £50 prize for the winning team. Maximum of four in a team. What do you think?'

'Can we get a team together?'

'Yes, I'm sure we can. Sandra and Ari are always up for a laugh and they know a lot of stuff, especially Ari does.'

'Yeah, true,' agreed Mark. 'OK, then, give 'em a call and see how they're fixed.'

Jane nodded, got up from the battered leather settee and walked over to the counter. There was no-one immediately available so she stood and looked round at the various cakes, offering themselves from beneath glass cloches. The carrot cake looked nice but the one she thought she'd go for was the three-layered coffee and walnut.

'Tempted?' The voice startled her a little.

'What?! No, no, not today, thank you, Brian,' she said, 'just the bill, please.'

'Yes, of course.' Brian busied himself retrieving the bill from its bulldog clip on the board and started to put the items into the till. 'Everything alright for you?' he asked idly but then spotted an unusual item. 'Who had the pigeon paté? Was it Mark?'

'Yes.'

'Enjoy it?' Brian looked up.

'Yes, yes, I believe so.' Jane looked across at Mark but decided he was too far away to shout and ask. 'Yes, yes, I'm sure he did.'

'It's a new thing. Just thought we'd try it out and see what the customers thought,' explained Brian. 'Seems to have gone down well.' He looked back at the bill. 'You just stuck to your usual buttered granary, then, Jane?'

'Stick with what you know, Brian, that's what I say – stick with what you know!' Brian raised his eyebrows but said nothing.

***

Sandra and Ari had been waiting on the corner when Jane pulled up. They got into the car, full of chatter and excitement for the evening ahead. They told the same story, in relays, of their preparations for tonight's quiz and of one previous such situation, when they had been on holiday in Alicante. Mark listened, attentively enough, but thought it wiser to maintain his teammates' expectations of his performance at a low level. He had found, throughout his life, that it was always better to under-promise. Jane could attest to that.

The Après Café was a little way from their village. It had once been a wayside inn, sitting as it did on a tight bend by a bridge over the Dent. The car parking was difficult to access and Mark had often thought that was one of the reasons it had failed as a pub. Anyway, it seemed to have found new life, now, as a café, and there were only two spaces left in the car park. Jane swung smoothly into the first of them.

As they crossed to the café, they divided into pairs and Ari started up a conversation about the weekend's rugby. Mark's understanding of rugby came from watching whereas Ari's came from playing and, although they both shared a love of the spectacle, they were sometimes divided in their opinions of what they had seen. Jane and Sandra were already deep into gossip about the recently-emerged affair between two married women in the village. Sandra's relish of the scandal was given added bite by a dalliance she, herself, had had ten years previously, and which was known to Jane but not to either of the men. Jane eyed her friend, as she listened, and thought how selective memories could be.

Mark reached the door first and went inside, followed by Ari. He turned instinctively to his right and took two steps forward before stopping abruptly. Ari almost collided with him. 'What's wrong?' he asked.

'There's someone in our seats,' Mark said.

'Which seats?' asked Ari, looking round at the three-quarters full café.

'The leather settees. We always sit on the leather settees and there's two people already sitting on them.'

Ari looked at Mark, who seemed paralysed by this unanticipated turn of events. Sandra and Jane had, by now, entered and were standing behind them. 'What's up?' asked Jane.

'There's people in our seats,' said Mark.

'Well, we'll have to find different ones, then, won't we?' said Jane breezily and walked past and over to a vacant table close to the leather settees. Sandra and Ari followed and sat down. Mark remained where he was, for a few seconds, before becoming slightly self-conscious and then making his way over to join his team.

'Drinks?' asked Ari, cheerily. 'What'll you have?'

'Let's get a bottle between us, shall we?' said Jane to Sandra. 'Usually works out cheaper.'

'Yes, fine,' said Sandra. 'Whatever white they've got.'

'Mark?' asked Ari.

'Oh, yes, sorry. I'll have an Urquell, if they've got it, or a Peroni, please.'

Ari stood. 'I'll come and give you a hand,' said Sandra, also standing, 'and have a look at what whites they've got.' They walked off to the bar.

'And let them know we've arrived!' called Mark to their retreating backs. Ari turned to face them. 'What name did you book it under?'

'It was by team name.' said Mark, 'We're the Settee

Set.' And with that, he favoured the couple on the leather settee with a blank stare, which only Jane noticed. The couple, themselves, were far too engrossed in lovey-dovey chitchat to pay any attention to the outside world, much less to Mark.

'Look!' said Jane in a stern sotto voce, 'they might not stay for the quiz and, if they don't, we can move over there. But, you should resign yourself to sitting here and get on with it. Don't spoil the evening over something so trivial.'

Mark looked at her and glowered. He knew she was right.

***

'Question number six,' said Brian, in a slightly formal manner, 'How many spots are there on twelve dice?'

Ari wrote down '252' on his piece of paper and showed it to Mark who was in charge (who had taken charge) of filling in the answer sheet. Mark looked at him and raised an eyebrow. 'Are you sure?' Ari nodded and made a wide-eyed face. He was confident. Mark wasn't. 'How many spots are there on one dice?' he asked.

'Twenty-one,' whispered Ari, 'six plus five plus four plus three plus two plus one,' Pause. 'And, technically, it's die, not dice.' Mark looked quizzically at him.

'That's right!' said Jane firmly and then mouthed 'twenty-one' to Mark.

'OK,' whispered Mark, 'and twenty-one times twelve is?'

'One twelve is twelve.' Despite its low volume, Jane's

voice still carried its sarcasm easily. 'Put down the two and carry the one,' she continued. 'Two twelves are twenty-four plus one is twenty-five. Put that down and what do you get? Two hundred and fifty-blood-two! Now is Ari, or is Ari not, a Maths professor at the university?'

'Yes, yes, of course he is. I didn't mean any disrespect. It's just that anyone can make a mistake and Ari did the calculation so quick.'

'Well, now you have your answer and we now know that Ari is both quick and accurate.'

'Yes, he is,' chimed Sandra. Mark looked at her for signs of humour but detected none.

'So, from now on, let's entrust all mathematical calculations to Ari and that's that.' Her tone was final. Mark knew that protest would yield nothing except tension. He whispered 'Sorry' to Ari and dutifully wrote '252' on the answer sheet.

The next few questions were answered collectively. Sandra knew Pascoe & Dalziel's first names [Andy & Pete]. Ari knew the names of the two Olympic cyclists who had got married in September [Jason Kenny and Laura Trott]. Mark knew what athletic achievement Tim Peake had accomplished whilst on the space station [ran the equivalent of the London Marathon] and Jane knew the stage names of Thomas Derbyshire and Robert Gardner [Cannon & Ball]. Nobody, however, knew what the world record was for the greatest number of kisses in one minute. Mark wrote down '10. Xxxx' on the bottom of the answer sheet.

'Question number eleven,' said Brian, in the same formal manner he had apparently felt the need to adopt for his role as quizmaster. 'What is seventeen cubed?'

All eyes turned to Ari. He wrote '4,913' on his piece of paper and turned it so that Mark could see it. Mark paused momentarily and glanced at Jane, whose eyes and nostrils flared. Mark wrote '4,913' on the answer sheet and gave it a quick nod. Ari flicked his piece of paper back towards himself and wrote on it: '289 x 17' and did the calculation. It came to 4,913, which he underlined. 'Thank God for that' he said and they all smiled.

The mid-session break arrived, after twenty questions, and, as if orchestrated, a file of young people, all dressed in black, emerged from the kitchen bearing trays of hot and cold food. 'If you just give the staff a couple of minutes, food will be served shortly,' announced Brian. 'In the meantime, I'll be bringing the bonus round sheet round for you to have a go at.'

'Drinks?' asked Mark. 'It's my round.'

'I think we're fine,' said Sandra, looking at Jane, who nodded.

'Snecklifter for me, then,' said Ari.

'Pint?' asked Mark.

Ari favoured him with an old-fashioned look. 'Pint it is, then,' said Mark, making off to the bar, at exactly the same moment as the man who was sitting on the leather settee rose and turned barwards. Mark quickened his step in an attempt to reach the bar first but the man had a long stride and stepped in front of the barmaid just as Mark got there. He half-turned. 'Oh sorry,' he offered without conviction. Mark said nothing and nursed his escalating resentment. 'There'll come a moment,' he thought.

When Mark returned to the table with the drinks, the other three were already tucking into their plates of meat pie, mushroom stroganoff or quiche. 'I wasn't sure what you'd want, so I didn't get you anything,' said Jane flatly. Mark looked at her momentarily but turned and went over to where the food was laid out.

There was only one other man there, putting bits and pieces onto a plate and most of the food dishes were at least half-empty. Mark sighed but picked up a plate and followed the man around the table. 'Oh well,' he thought, 'time to experiment.' He spooned stroganoff and meat pie together onto his plate. The chips had all gone but there was plenty of crispy kale and green beans to be had. He walked back to the table without enthusiasm.

'Come on,' said Ari, encouragingly, on his return, 'we have to identify which ten out of these twenty countries is bigger than the UK.'

'Got any yet?' asked Mark.

'Well, yes, the obvious ones – Germany, Finland, Poland and Syria – but there's some really tricky ones. New Zealand, Japan, The Phillipines. What do you think?'

Mark was about to query Syria but then, picturing it on a map, thought that maybe it had a lot of desert. After all, Algeria was a huge country, dipping down into the Sahara. Maybe Syria was the same and they wouldn't call it 'The Syrian Desert' if it wasn't quite extensive. But, as well as all that, he didn't really want to challenge Ari again and he *was* Kurdish, from that neck of the woods. No, best to keep shtum for now and wait and see if an opportunity might arise later. 'Don't know about those,' he said, 'although I think New Zealand's fractionally bigger but that's from third year Geography.'

Jane and Sandra were paying no attention. They were having a who-said-what-to-who conversation centred around one of Sandra's work colleagues and it almost seemed rude to interrupt.

'So, girls, what do you think?' asked Mark loudly. 'Which is bigger, the UK or Japan?'

They both stopped talking immediately and Jane looked sharply at Mark. 'We were just…' she began but was interrupted by Sandra.

'I think I know this,' she said. 'Although it never looks it on the globe, Japan's a bit bigger. Got lots of islands, see. Honshu, the main island is slightly smaller than Great Britain, our main island, but, of course, when you add in all the other islands, that makes it bigger. We're less than 100,000sq miles and they're nearer 150,000.'

There was a moment of stunned silence as Mark, Jane and especially Ari stared at Sandra. It was broken only by the couple at the next table breaking into spontaneous applause. Sandra looked over at them, smiled broadly, and nodded. 'We had a training day at work,' she explained.

***

'And, finally, question number forty,' said Brian, 'which US state has the lowest population density?'

Sandra, who had lived in the US for five years, was, at that moment, in the toilet. Ari, Mark and Jane looked at each other but none of them made an immediate response.

'Could be one of those states in the Midwest – Wyoming or Montana – somewhere like that,' offered Ari.

'Yes, those places that cowboys ride through, with pointy mountains and flat desert plains. Never seems like anybody lives there,' Mark agreed.

'Course, who we need here is Sandra. She flew all over the States when she lived there. But where is she when we need her? In the toilet!' said Ari.

Jane rose to her feet and nodded in the direction of the toilets. 'I'll ask 'er,' she said and walked off.

Ari and Mark looked at each other, without speaking. Both were mentally consulting their maps of the US in search of likely cool spots for population but neither felt confident to offer any further opinion, especially in light of Sandra knowing the likely answer. Best to wait. Mark wrote '40. US state' on the bottom of the answer sheet.

'Let's put in some more of these countries bigger than the UK,' suggested Ari, finally.

'OK, why don't we all put in our guesses and then go with the majority?'

'Yes, good idea,' said Ari, 'aggregating socially distributed information to obtain intelligent outcomes'

Mark looked at him blankly and Ari smiled and waved his hand, as if to say 'What am I like?' although, of course, he would never utter a sentence like that. Mark looked at the list and put a tick against his guesses. He did not include Syria. He passed the paper over to Ari, who examined carefully each possibility before deciding whether to put a dot next to it or not. He had just finished when the women returned from the toilet. They were discussing Sandra's work colleague again.

'These countries,' said Ari brightly to the women, 'what we thought was that, if we all put down our guesses, we'll see which are the most popular and go with those.' Both Sandra and Jane looked straight at Ari whilst they processed his statement.

'Oh,' said Jane, 'let's just go with what you two have come up with.' She looked at Sandra for confirmation, which Sandra gave, with a shrug. Ari and Mark had both been in situations like this with their wives before, and knew it was best not to quibble.

Ari looked at the list. 'Well, between us, it looks like we agree on Germany, Finland, Poland, New Zealand, the Phillipines, and Vietnam but, then we'll have to decide between the other eight and pick four.'

'You choose two and I'll choose two,' said Mark firmly, and that's what they did. Sandra and Jane took no interest, being too absorbed in office politics to worry about such an urgent matter.

***

'Right,' said Barry loudly, 'if you'd like to swap your main answer sheet with someone at an adjacent table, we'll get down to the answers.'

'We still need answers to these two!' Mark said urgently.

'Which two?' asked Ari.

'World record for kisses in a minute. US state with fewest people.'

'Some people can kiss very quickly,' said Sandra, looking at Ari, who shook his head almost imperceptibly. 'Maybe 120, then,' said Jane, 'that'd be twice a second.'

'I'd go for 150, then,' said Sandra, 'it's a world record so they can probably go even faster than that.' She nodded at Mark, who dutifully wrote down '148,' just to make it not look like a guess.

'And the last one is,' Mark continued, 'the US state with the lowest population.'

'Oh, that's Wyoming,' Sandra said, 'very little there but cattle and plains.' Jane nodded once more at Mark, who duly wrote down 'Wyoming.'

Mark reached over and tapped the arm of the woman sitting at the next table. 'Swap?' he enquired brightly. 'Oh, we've already swapped,' she said and nodded in the direction of the lovebirds on the settee.

'Well, we could do a three-way,' he said looking the woman dead in the eye but without flinching.

'Suppose so,' she said reluctantly and placed into Mark's hand, the answer sheet of the team named 'Twogether.' He pointed out the name to Ari and made the gesture of putting his fingers down his throat. Ari smiled amiably but said nothing.

'So firstly,' announced Brian, 'the countries larger than

the UK.' He proceeded to read them out, in alphabetical order, as they were on the sheet. They scored 8/10. Mark noted, with some small satisfaction, that Syria, one of Ari's choices, had not made the list. 'Doesn't know everything,' thought Mark.

Brian then started through the answers to the questions in the main quiz. Mark sat with his pen poised to place a tick or cross next to Twogether's answers and Ari looked on. It seemed to Ari as if Mark's pen carried rather more flourish into the crosses, than the ticks. Sandra and Jane paid scant attention to this part of the proceedings, deep in conversation as they were, over the merits of different ski resorts.

'252' and '4913' were, indeed, correct answers and they had even managed 'MMMMCMXIII' as the response to putting '4913' into Roman numerals. Mark had thought, at the time, that the question was rather unfair – you couldn't get the second question right if you had got the first wrong – but now that they, courtesy of Ari, had got it right and Twogether had it wrong, he found himself less resentful.

The world record for the most kisses in a minute turned out to be 258, a fact which suddenly brought Sandra and Jane back down the pistes and into the Après café. 'I don't believe that,' said Sandra, 'that's more than four kisses a second. Impossible!' And then, without pausing, she turned to Jane. 'Ere, come 'ere,' she said and leaned over to her. 'Ari, count these,' she commanded and started kissing Jane, on the lips, as fast as she could.

Jane's reaction was described to her, later, by Mark, as a mixture of disbelief and revulsion, although that wasn't what she remembered feeling at the time. What she remembered was that everyone would be looking at her (they were) and that she should try to pass it off as just a bit of fun (she didn't). When Sandra finally stopped, she remained frozen in her chair for a number of seconds, with her eyes still tight shut and her hands gripping the edge of the table.

'How many was that?' Sandra asked Ari.

'Thirty-seven,' said Ari

'And how long?'

'Sixteen seconds,' said Ari.

'So, how many's that a minute? she asked.

'About 140,' estimated Ari before Mark was able to confirm, using his phone, that it was just over 138 kisses per minute. 'See,' said Sandra, 'impossible!' and surveyed the entire café with the assuredness borne of partial knowledge and two glasses of wine. Those other quizzers who were still looking at her, turned back to their answer sheets.

'Shall I continue?' asked Brian to a rousing affirmative hum. He made his way, methodically, through the remaining questions until he arrived at the final question. 'So, Question forty,' he said, 'the US state with the lowest population density is… Alaska.'

'What?!' said Mark, looking directly at Sandra. Sandra had been quiet for a while, reflecting on the wisdom of her little demonstration and whether it had, in any way, harmed her friendship with Jane, but she was brought back into the here-and-now by Mark's question. 'You said 'Wyoming,'' he accused.

'Wyoming is the state with the lowest population,' said Sandra 'and that, I believe, is what you said the question was.'

'Population density was what the question was,' said Ari.

'Oh, that's Alaska,' said Sandra glibly.

Mark was incensed that they had conspired to make such a mistake when expertise was so clearly to hand but, if he was honest, he couldn't now remember exactly what question he had posed to Sandra. He fumed quietly but, then, couldn't suppress a scoff as he looked at Twogether's answer sheet and there, next to the number forty, was their answer: Alaska.

He pushed their sheet away from him and it was left to Ari to take it and tot up their score. He stood and returned the sheet to the couple. The girl took it without breaking eye contact with the man. 'Thanks.' Their answer sheet came back from the adjacent table with a 'thirty-five' ringed in red at the top.

'So,' said Brian, 'add together your mark from the main quiz with your mark out of ten from the countries quiz.'

'Right,' said Mark, 'we got thirty-five plus eight: forty-three.'

Ari smiled his acknowledgement and nodded. Sandra and Jane looked nonplussed and returned to a conversation about salopettes v ski trousers.

'Finally,' said Brian, 'take off one point for every member in your team.'

'What?!' Mark was again in a state between 'taken-aback' and 'fury.' 'Take off a point for every team member? I don't remember reading anything about that.' Ari shrugged. Sandra looked at him blankly, and, Jane said, 'Oh, just do it. It's to help even out the teams.'

Mark stared, for a while, took a deep breath in and wrote 'thirty-nine' at the top of the sheet. 'Yes, that's right,' said Ari, completely unnecessarily. Mark stared straight ahead. Sandra and Jane continued their sartorial comparisons.

'Now, then,' said Brian, after the hubbub had settled down, 'please put your hand up if you've got a score above forty-five.' Mark could hardly bear to look and was relieved to see no hand raised.

'Any mark above forty,' asked Brian. Again no hand raised. Mark felt a whoop of excitement grip his chest. Now, he was certain, they had an unbeatable score and he didn't need Ari to confirm that. He glanced over at Ari to find him, irritatingly, beaming.

'Anything over thirty-five?' asked Brian and Mark's hand shot into the air. His was the only such hand and he started to anticipate the £12.50 coming his way. He had, temporarily forgotten, the tenner Jane had demanded off him the previous week, so £12.50 or, as he liked to convert it, three pints of Urquell, seemed like riches. He could almost taste the lager when, from across the room came a woman's voice: 'Oh, yes, and us two (she smiled at her partner as she said this) over thirty-five.' Mark let out a sigh he hoped no-one heard.

'So,' said Brian, 'how many?'

'Thirty-nine,' said the young woman and Mark in perfect chorus.

'Well,' said Brian, 'couldn't be more of a dead-heat than that, could it? How exciting! Now we'll have to have a tie-breaker. It's one question and the nearest to the right answer wins. OK?' Mark nodded and the girl from the settee said, distractedly, 'Yeah, OK.'

'They only got thirty-one, right, before, so that means they must have got all ten of the countries right,' whispered Mark to Ari. 'Doesn't seem likely.'

'Well,' said Ari, 'we can't do anything about that now. Let's see what the tie-breaker is and who has the best idea.' Mark shook his head slightly and swilled the last of his lager. Sandra and Jane paused their conversation and leant forwards across the table.

'Right,' announced Brian, 'ready for the tie-breaker? Write down your answers on a piece of paper with your team names on the top and bring it up to me. Nearest wins. OK? Here's the question: How many British No.1 hits has Madonna had?'

'Right,' said Ari, 'what do we all think?'

'She's been going to ages, more than thirty years and she's always releasing stuff,' said Mark, 'so my guess would be over thirty. One a year, that sort of thing.'

'Yes,' said Sandra, 'but it might not always have been the case that they got to No.1. Everyone remembers 'Holiday' but it only ever reached No.2 in the UK. And my favourite, 'Ray of Light' – only ever No.2 over here. I don't know exactly how many but I bet it's a smaller number than you think.'

There was a moment of silence amongst the others as they took in Sandra's analysis. Eventually, Ari said, 'So, what would you say?'

'Fifteen'd be my guess,' said Sandra, authoritatively.

'Are we all alright with that?' Ari checked round his teammates' faces. Two nods. He wrote 'fifteen' and 'The Settee Set' on a piece of paper and took it up to where Brian was perched. He went back and sat down. There was much giggling and playful touching on the settee and their answer took a little longer to emerge. Finally, though, a piece of paper was placed in Brian's hand.

'OK, ladies and gentlemen,' said Brian. 'Thank you for your patience and I'm pleased to say, we have a winner.' He unfolded the first piece of paper. Mark could see, even from the distance across the café, that it was theirs. Was that a bad sign?

'The Settee Set, even though they're not actually sitting on the settee, have said 'fifteen.' There were murmurings around the other tables. Mark tried to look stony-faced. 'The Twogether team have said 'sixteen.' Increased murmurings and an upsurge of conversation. Brian held his hands up to appeal, silently, for quiet.' It seems, ladies and gentlemen, as if these two teams are almost inseparable,' he said.

'So, what's the answer?' piped up someone from the far reaches of the café.

Mark was almost numb with anticipation. He knew, deep in his bones, that Madonna, had had more hits than fifteen and that, just as everything else this evening had gone against him, this would, too. And this time, there'd be no wriggling out of the blame for Sandra. No-one else had said 'fifteen.' That was her number. 'Oh, God,' he thought, 'why didn't I speak up? Flopsy and Mopsy are about to run off with twenty-five quid each and it's all because we listened to Sandra. I don't really know why we invited them in the first place – it was all Jane's idea.'

In fact, Mark was so preoccupied with his pre-emptive recriminations that he completely missed Brian's announcement:

'Twelve.'

The Bedside Café

Iona's the sister of Arlo
And Arlo's the brother of Gus.
On journeys, they make quite a carload
And at home, they make quite a fuss.

One day, when they'd been to their aunties'
And came home all filled up with sweets,
They changed quick and kicked off their panties
And all round the home they did leap.

Their dad said, 'Oh do please be quiet
And please take those pants off your head.'

Their mum said, 'Stop making a riot
And calm down or you'll go to bed.'

'Find something to do all together
Find something that makes little noise,
So be a good girl now, Iona,
Find something to do with the boys.'

Iona went off to her bedroom
And wanted to do what Mum said,
And although there wasn't much headroom
She made them all sit on the bed.

She went first to look for her tea set
The kettle, the cups and the pot.
Then saucepans and spoons she had to get
And those were the things that she got.

The third thing she got was some biscuits
The fourth thing she got was some cake.
She thought about juice – should she risk it?
Then thought of the mess it might make.

By this time the boys were quite wriggly
And wanted to help set it up,
But Arlo was feeling quite giggly
And Gus was a proper muck pup.

'Sit still!' she commanded her brothers
'You're being as loud as can be!'
Her voice was the same as her mother's
And made poor Gus want to go wee.

She stood back and looked at the layout

All pretty and really quite gay,
Then turned round and gave out a loud shout
'Come look now, I've made a café.'

Her parents came in and they sat down
Next to the bunk bed, on the floor,
The waitress was in a dressing gown
The boys only pants, nothing more.

'I like this a lot,' said mum Lucy
'I like this a lot,' said dad Brode,
'I'd like to eat something quite juicy'
'It's biscuits or cake!' he was told.

They all ate the food they were given
They all drank the drink – though pretend.
They cuddled together, like heaven

They hoped that it would never end.

... and it never did.